SWEET CHARDONNAY

A sweet, mature, small town romance

LYZ KELLEY

Belvitri
Services

A special gift just for you.

I have a present for you...

...your very own ebook exclusive when you sign up for my newsletter.

Newsletter Sign Up
https://geni.us/LyzKelleyFreeBook

Chapter 1

The dread plaguing Sherry Kline since the day she'd received the Employee of the Year award notice had escalated to a point that she wondered if she needed to have a cardiologist on speed dial. She stood in the open doorway of her walk-in closet, next to her daughter, tension slowly knotting her muscles and tendons with every tick of the old-fashioned wall clock. She'd been avoiding this moment for weeks but could no longer put off planning for the company awards ceremony she was required to attend. She wrung her hands and moved away from her daughter.

"Mom, please stop pacing already." Alison grasped Sherry's hand, gently tugging her back to the closet entrance. "I know you're anxious about the trip, but it will be fine. More than fine. A week at a luxurious hotel will be fun, and you deserve this getaway."

Twenty-three-year-old Alison was the mirror image of her father. She had his deep brown eyes and copper-red hair, a lovely blend of red and bronze. Then again, Alison had Sherry's height and stood at an average five-six with slender shoulders on top of a petite frame. Too bad John never got to see his daughter graduate from college and wouldn't be there to walk her down the marriage aisle or hold his grandbabies Alison boasted she'd have one day.

Alison stepped into the narrow closet, her gaze searching one end to the other. She shook her head as she trailed her fingers over tailored gray pants, white cotton blouses, and black skirts. "You should have gone shopping for this trip, Mom. What you have here are work clothes. There's no way you can wear any of these to an employee appreciation event. Plus, it's a five-star resort. You need something fancier."

Yet another reason she didn't want to attend.

A slight tremor went through Sherry, her body tightening. She curved her hand around the back of her neck, digging her fingers into the muscles to loosen them.

"My clothes are fine, darling." Sherry rubbed her arms as if to wipe off a chill. The thought of packing for California was making her crazy.

Working on a project plan, following up on past due tasks, and sorting out problems was much easier than traveling halfway across the US for an event she had not voluntarily signed up for. Yes, winning the Employee of the Year Award for her company division was an honor, but still, she'd prefer a simple plaque to display on her desk.

As a global insurance company with offices around the world, Stallion Protection Partners relied on events like the annual ceremony to bolster corporate pride and loyalty. Every year, divisional honorees were treated to a company-sponsored vacation at an exclusive destination and a huge banquet where the company bigwigs handed out awards and made speeches, or so Sherry had heard.

The all-expense-paid trip this year was being hosted at the Silver Fox Resort, a stunning property situated on more than four hundred acres of rugged California coastline. The top thirty divisional winners would attend with their significant other or a guest.

Sherry was forced to attend the event by herself as neither Alison nor her son, Tyler, were available to accompany her. She was facing a social setting with individuals she only knew from a business setting. With nineteen separate units comprising a workforce of more than 2,500 employees within the US division alone, she wouldn't know more than a handful of people, all of whom she'd interacted with on a purely professional basis.

As project manager, she thrived within the boundaries of her role. Expectations and etiquette were clearly defined in the workspace, and she wasn't obligated to share personal details. She could interact with people without being subjected to pitying looks and stilted conversations.

Desperate to shake off her identity as a poor, lonely, grief-stricken widow, she'd poured all of her energy into building a career that enabled her to take care of Alison and Tyler, helping both of them with college expenses and getting them launched into the world. Not only was she reluctant to mingle with coworkers, she'd begun to realize that one day—sooner than later—her kids would be completely independent and would no longer need her help.

Sherry's gaze strayed to the window, taking in the sunlight streaming into her bedroom. Any other day, the golden rays would have soothed her mood, but today she was too agitated to appreciate the beauty.

She'd be forced to reinvent herself yet again, and she didn't have a clue who she was or who she wanted to be.

"Earth to Mom." Alison stepped in front of Sherry, waving her hands. "Are you listening to me?"

Sherry grimaced, her shoulders drooping as she turned away from the window. Her resistance to stepping out of her deeply grooved rut was the reason she'd put off the packing.

But if she didn't pack now, she might forget something critical, like her underwear. She hated putting things off to the last minute, and procrastination wasn't usually her style.

"I'm sorry. I got distracted." Sherry couldn't help the cold tremors tumbling though her body. "You have my full attention now."

"Mom? What's wrong?"

"It's just this trip." She forced a smile to ease the worry on her daughter's face. "It's going to be hard for me. I've never been to California or attended such a big executive function —at least not one where I had to go on my own."

"I understand more than you think, Mom. I remember the first day you dropped me off my freshman year of high school. I was terrified. What if I didn't wear the right clothes or talk to the right people? Good thing I was distracted and slammed into Claire. That chance meeting saved us both."

The funny, quirky-yet-shy Claire became Alison's best friend that fateful day. The two were like having a set of twins around. The pair wore the same clothes, told the same jokes, and were drawn to the same type of boys, although Sherry had heard them pinky swear never to date each other's ex-boyfriends.

If only life were that simple.

Sherry acknowledged her daughter's statement with a nod, but her stomach churned with worry. She swallowed the bile rising in her throat, trying to appear cheerful since she didn't want her daughter to worry, and then wandered over to the window.

"Mom, you're pacing again." Alison's brows furrowed.

She hadn't been this unnerved since her first day on the job with her recently earned project manager certificate in hand. Thank goodness, John's life insurance had given her enough to finish her degree and get back into the workforce.

Nothing had made her as nauseous as going on this

seven-day corporate vacation except the morning sickness she had with her oldest. Tyler had given her fits the entire nine months, from a constantly queasy stomach, to flipping and flopping, to arriving so fast she and John barely made it to the hospital. As a young man, he was still the same—minus the heartburn and unsettled stomach—always on the go, always daring something new and exciting. He was twenty-five now and still had the same driven personality.

Where had the time gone? She'd put off the inevitable long enough.

"Let's get this packing over with." She lifted a long strand of her daughter's hair, letting the silky smoothness distract her.

"Yet packing is going to be harder than I thought," Alison said. "How about we go shopping? We still have time. A couple of hours at the mall trying on new outfits might get you excited for the trip."

"I'd rather not. I hate those cramped dressing rooms. Besides, I don't want to stand in front of a mirror and see all my cellulite and wrinkles or try fifty dresses on only to find not one of them fits." It was a thin excuse and she'd probably regret not taking her daughter's advice, but this trip represented so much more than an uncomfortable corporate event. "I'll add a scarf or some jewelry to my office suits."

"Mom!" Alison performed a perfect eye roll. "Not a single item here is appropriate for your trip. Since you won't go shopping, we need to come up with another plan. You deserve this honor. You've been working hard these past few years. I don't know how you manage to work fifty hours a week, maintain the house, pay bills, handle all the responsibilities Dad used to take care of, and still be there for Tyler and me."

Alison made it sound like Sherry had consciously chosen to become a super woman. In truth, she'd gathered up the shattered pieces of their lives and done her best to reassemble them into a new normal.

"Oh, alright. I'm open to a few suggestions. But make it fast. I bought a nice bottle of Chardonnay to share." Warm pleasure triggered by Alison's admiration displaced some of Sherry's anxiety. "I'll do your nails, and you can do mine while we enjoy a nice glass of wine together."

"Awesome idea, Mom. We haven't had time to just hang out and do girly things in months. I'm so busy at work, and every weekend we're focused on making your organic bath products. I'm not complaining. I just wish there were more hours in the day." Alison's brows lifted. "You have no excuse, though, not to have met with your friends for lunch or at least ventured out to your favorite nursery for new plants and flowers. Spring is your favorite season. You should be celebrating the change of season, especially after the tough winter we had. I heard the weatherman say it was one of Iowa's worst."

She flinched, surprised Alison had noticed. Everything changed when John died, and while her heart was still beating, sometimes it felt like part of her died with him. She hated the cautious way her friends asked questions, as if they didn't want to upset her, much like the whispered sympathies she got at his funeral. Gardening was something they'd done together. Without him...

"I'll make time to do all those things when I get back."

"You promise? Because you haven't used any of your time off, and you rarely treat yourself to a lazy day. If anyone deserves this award, it's you. I sincerely hope you're able to relax and enjoy this trip. "Alison reached into the lower part of the closet, slipping out two battered suitcases, and huffed, her forehead creasing as a thoughtful look settled on her face.

Sherry laughed at her daughter's reaction. "Don't say it."

"I can't help it, Mom. These suitcases are gross. I can't let you take these cruddy old things to the resort. My luggage is brand new. I don't mind loaning it to you since I'm not going to use it anytime soon."

"No, I can't take yours. You bought that set to go on vacation with Derrick before you had to reschedule. Just four more weeks until he's done with his master's degree, and then you can plan a getaway." Oh, to be young again.

Remembering the first trip she and John had taken as newlyweds filled her with wistful longing. They'd been talking about where to go when he finally retired, but that, along with so many other plans, would never happen now.

"My suitcases are fine. No one's going to see them."

"Mom, please." Alison's voice was soft, a mix of concern, frustration, and annoyance. "Why can't you just accept my help? I don't care if the suitcases get a little banged up. It will happen eventually, whether on your trip or mine."

"Okay." Sherry realized turning down Alison's help and putting off packing wasn't going to get her out of this trip. She needed to confront the situation, just like she'd handled everything else after John died. When the grief and despair threatened to suck her under, focusing on Tyler and Alison kept her going.

Love for her children swelled in her heart. "What did I ever do to have been blessed with such a wonderful daughter?"

"I am wonderful, aren't I." Alison pretended to preen, and they both giggled.

Oh, to have such confidence again.

Alison's eyes widened as if a brilliant idea had occurred to her. "If you won't go shopping at the mall, you can shop in my closet. I have the perfect outfit for you to wear to the welcome reception."

At the mention of the dreaded event, with non-stop

activities, Sherry's middle twisted again. "Let's search through my stuff again. I have a few nice dresses. They'll work fine."

"No, they won't." Alison dashed out of the room, calling from her bedroom across the hall. "Let me grab a few things."

She returned with a large suitcase still encased in protective plastic and clothes draped over one arm. She laid out several dresses, beige pants, and three designer blouses. Last to be added to the lineup was a teal-blue bathing suit.

Sherry choked at the sight of the bikini. "I'm not wearing that."

"Look, it has a skirted bottom, and you can use this sarong to cover up." Alison fumbled in the pile for a colorful swath of fabric. "It has plenty of coverage, and you still have a nice figure. At least take it with you."

"What about all this other stuff?" Sherry lifted a white maxi dress by the straps, a price tag fluttering from the armhole. "You've never even worn this."

"I got these dresses and the bathing suit a few months ago when Claire and I went on a shopping spree. I thought they'd be nice for my trip to Mexico with Derrick." Alison tore off the wrappings around the suitcase. "It's no big deal. Besides, I want you to relax and indulge yourself."

Sherry held the dress up to gauge the fit. "This is way too revealing. I might be going to a resort, but I'll be interacting with coworkers."

"This is what women wear to a place like the Silver Fox Resort." Alison took the white maxi and handed her another dress. "Try this blue one. I have a coordinating linen blazer. It might be a good choice in case the temperature drops."

At least this one covered most of her skin.

Alison rummaged in Sherry's closet and came back with shoes, scarves, and a straw sun hat. "See. Not such a big deal to put together a wardrobe for seven days of fun."

"Wow. I forgot I still had that old thing." Sherry reached out and smoothed a finger over the black ribbon band.

"You wore that on your anniversary cruise." Alison set it on Sherry's head. "There's a picture of you and Dad where the hat is almost flying off. I love that shot."

For a moment, Sherry just *remembered*.

Her gaze drifted around the bedroom, unchanged since John's death. The only things that stood out as new were the hand-labeled bottles and jars containing her organic lotions and creams. A thrilling sense of satisfaction displaced her concern about the trip as she spotted the newest batch of homemade organic shampoo in a basket on her dresser.

No matter how many hours she worked during the week, Saturday and Sunday were dedicated to her hobby. She'd resumed making organic soaps and body butters a few months after losing John, needing a distraction to pull her out of her sorrow. She was fascinated by the process and spent hours researching organic elements and concocting her own recipes. When creating, testing, and experimenting, she was at peace.

Once upon a time, she'd dreamed of owning an organic cosmetics company, but marriage and motherhood came first, and that fantasy had been packed up and forgotten. Rediscovering her passion had been a lifesaver.

"By the way, Ali, I noticed you straightened my room this morning while I was making breakfast." Sherry tapped her daughter's shoulder. The duvet was tucked in and pillows stacked. The TV remote control and charging station were lined up, side by side. The dirty clothes basket was empty, indicating Alison had taken her laundry downstairs. "You don't need to take care of me, honey."

"Blame it on the good habits you ingrained in me as a child." Alison avoided her eyes. "You were the one who made me clean my room every week."

"Oh, so your cleaning habits are my fault," Sherry teased.

"Isn't everything the mother's fault?" Alison held up one of the blouses piled on the bed. "What do you think about this one?"

The chocolate-colored fabric with gold bead trim matched the color of Alison's eyes.

"It's a bit…flashy. Don't you think it's too young for me?"

"Mom! You are not old." Alison mock-frowned. "Grandma is old."

"Good thing Nanna didn't hear you or she would give you a piece of her mind. She says seventy-five is the new fifty-five."

"She's right. You need to remember your life isn't over just because Dad is gone. You're healthy and active. You deserve happiness." Alison neatly folded the shirt and added it to the suitcase, ticking off the various items she'd packed. "You'll look fabulous in any of these dresses. I'll pack extra so you have options."

Options? Sherry almost snorted. It didn't feel like she had many options, especially those of the self-indulgent type. Since becoming a widow, Sherry had felt the strain of her limitations. Once she paid off the mortgage and funeral expenses, there wasn't much left. After decades as a stay-at-home-mom, Sherry had been thrust back into the workforce so she could provide for herself and help Tyler and Alison. The dramatic change had left her dizzy. Luckily, she'd been able to hang onto the family home and they had each other. And, once she got accustomed to the new routine, she found her job rewarding and fulfilling in a way she hadn't expected.

"The resort is beautiful. Aren't you the least bit excited?" Alison closed the suitcase but didn't latch it. "Claire and I looked up their website, and now she wants to have her wedding there."

"That's a bit premature, considering she isn't dating

anyone." The photos of the Silver Fox Resort showed well-tended gardens, rustic luxury, a vineyard, a high-end spa, a fully outfitted gym and pool, and breathtaking ocean views. If she wasn't dreading the social portion of the trip, she'd already be packed and counting down the days until she checked in.

Thinking about the award ceremony and the requirement to interact with coworkers in a casual setting made her stomach roll like the wicked drop of a roller coaster. Sherry wrapped her arms around her waist and shivered.

"You're tensing up again, Mom. Relax. Why are you so nervous? I'm sure your colleagues are very nice people. This will give you a chance to hob-nob with the top executives and maybe get that pay raise you deserve. Stop worrying."

Stop worrying, she says. She doesn't understand the other award winners will be there with their spouses or a family member or...someone significant. I'll stick out like a sore thumb.

"Mom?" Alison touched her elbow, bringing Sherry out of her dark thoughts.

"I'm fine, honey."

"No, you aren't. Tell me what has you so on edge about this trip?"

"Okay, I'll admit it. I'm nervous about meeting new people. Socializing was your father's bailiwick, not mine." Sherry sank onto the edge of the bed.

As a widow, she tried her best to blend in during office Christmas parties and company picnics, but this time around she wouldn't be with friends—more like acquaintances. Other men and women her age were single but being widowed in her forties made her feel like she had a huge neon sign over her head announcing it to the world.

The awards event would be different than casual office gatherings because she anticipated most people would be paired off while she was attending by herself. She would see those happy couples and be reminded of the wonderful man she lost. She would see them walking through the gardens hand in hand, enjoying intimate candlelight dinners in the resort restaurant, and—worst of all—embracing and celebrating when the awards were handed out. She wouldn't go unnoticed, but it was unwanted attention. Sympathy and pity for the lonely widow. Some might be kind enough to ask her to tag along, while others would give her a wide berth, not sure what to say.

She didn't want pity. She didn't need it, and she would never accept it. She'd immersed herself in her job to fill the gap created by John's absence. Her kids and her hobby kept her sane, kept her motivated, and kept her content.

"It will be okay, Mom." Alison sat down next to her and curved her arm around Sherry's shoulders. "Remember how nervous I was on my first day of elementary school? I hid in the bathroom because I was afraid and didn't want to go, but you found me and made me realize how much fun I'd be missing out on and that all the other kids were just as unsure. You are amazing. I've always looked up to you. It's okay to be nervous but think about the fun you'll be missing if you don't go, or worse, stay in your room all day. If anyone deserves this vacation, it's you."

"That's sweet of you to say, honey. I'm surprised you remember the exact words I used on your first day of elementary school two decades ago." She took a deep breath. "I just don't know what to expect, and I need predictability in my life right now."

"We've all struggled, and it's sad Dad isn't here to share this achievement with you. He'd be very proud," Alison said.

"Going on this trip doesn't feel like a reward for winning Employee of the Year," Sherry grumbled. "The corporate CEO from headquarters in Australia will be there, and I'll spend my time worrying if I have lipstick on my teeth or garlic on my breath. I wish you or Tyler could go with me, but I understand you both have other obligations."

Alison set her hand on Sherry's. "Dad wouldn't want you sitting on the sidelines. You have to get back to living."

When did the mother-daughter roles become reversed? My babies have grown up. Before too long, Alison and Tyler will have their own families. This house will be way too quiet.

Sherry's heart jumped into her throat as anxiety again knotted her guts.

The house no longer had sports playing on the television, or the echo of another person talking on the phone, or someone chopping vegetables for dinner. She hated being surrounded by silence and worked to fill the time honing her organic products.

But she wasn't one to back away from a challenge.

If she could make it through John's death, she could get through this corporate event without making a fool of herself. Plus, there was another, maybe even more vital, reason she overcome her social anxiety—job security.

People were whispering about staff cuts. Nothing specific and nothing she could confirm, but with enough detail to lend credence to the rumors. If the company downsized, she didn't want to be one of the people out of a job.

She needed predictability and stability and her job met the need. She'd found a new comfort zone. The day job didn't fulfill her like her hobby creating organic beauty products did, but at least she wasn't pacing around a too-quiet house or crying over photo albums anymore.

Maybe attending this dreaded affair would prove she was a team player and score points with Wade Briggs, head of the North American office. A casual conversation over appetizers might provide an opportunity to remind him of her cost-saving contributions to the company and find out if the rumors were fact or fiction.

Fear of losing her job provided the motivation she needed to get through this company-mandated getaway.

"Thanks for helping me pack. I feel a little less overwhelmed now, although I'm not wearing that bikini." Sherry resigned herself to enduring seven days at a beautiful resort...in the company of paired-off coworkers.

"Promise you'll try to have a good time." Alison shifted to look Sherry in the face, the concerned dip of her brows emphasizing the importance of her request. "We've all dealt with losing Dad in different ways. What I miss about him is different than what Tyler misses. Losing Dad was hard, but I can't imagine what it's like to lose someone who wasn't only a husband but your best friend and partner and main support. You've been ignoring your grief to help us cope, and that's not healthy. Enjoying this trip is an important step in your healing, Mom."

"Look at you, so grown up." Sherry blinked away the tears stinging the backs of her eyes. Alison had put into words what Sherry felt in her heart and couldn't express. "I'll finish packing my toiletries and personal items later because I think I hear that bottle of Chardonnay calling."

Alison burst into laughter and gave her a hug.

Even if the trip was horrible, Sherry would be coming home to her amazing, wonderful children. In the grand scheme of things, family was the only thing that really mattered.

Chapter 2

*A*t the sound of a sharp knock, Wade Briggs dragged his eyes from his computer screen and pushed back from his desk. He'd been at work for well over three hours, and his shoulders already ached with tension. "Come in."

"Here you go, Mr. Briggs." Kimberly Warwick, Wade's assistant, breezed into the office. She balanced a Starbucks cup in one hand and a stack of folders and binders in the crook of her elbow. She placed the coffee on his desk. "Black, two creams, no sugar. Is there anything else you need?"

"Thanks." He shook his head, fighting back a yawn, and then stretched his arms overhead, feeling the pull of each sore muscle. Too many hours at his desk was showing itself in aches and pains. "The good news is that a replacement coffee machine will be installed tomorrow. You won't have to go down the street to get coffee for me anymore."

"I don't mind getting your mid-morning coffee. Springtime in Denver can be hit or miss, but it's been beautiful all week. I like getting out. It's a nice break and gives me time to prioritize the rest of my day." Her bright smile dimmed as she shifted to a more professional demeanor. "I only have a few more details to confirm for the employee awards event. Everything has fallen into place nicely."

"Thanks for the hard work you've put into planning and organizing this year's getaway. The location is ideal for our purposes. Rest and relaxation for the top-performing employees with plenty of opportunities to interact and strengthen professional relationships in a laidback atmosphere." Wade removed the lid, inhaling the brew's robust scent, instantly feeling reenergized. He took a careful sip, sighing in satisfaction. "Is the employee activity list ready?"

"I've got it right here." She pulled out a blue binder.

"Why don't you take a seat? We'll review the list now so if I get dragged into another meeting, I won't hold you up. It seems like some of the planning committee members are waiting on the information."

"Sounds great." Kimberly settled into one of the cream-colored fabric chairs in front of Wade's desk and stacked the pile of items she'd carried in with her onto the other chair. "It'll only take a moment to review the updates to the list."

Wade took another sip of coffee as his assistant struggled to keep loose pages together in an overstuffed three-inch binder.

"I meant to add these pages, but I can't get the rings open." Balancing the heavy notebook on her lap, she pressed on the tab to pop the rings open, but they remained clamped together.

Wade resisted the urge to volunteer his assistance. The latches could be tricky, especially when there were too many sheets in the binder. He tended to be a fixer but had learned the importance of allowing people, employees included, to figure things out themselves. He was more than willing to help if asked, but problem-solving was an important skill only mastered through firsthand experience.

Today, however, his patience was stretched thin—too thin —with dozens of critical decisions to be made and not enough time to deal with everything that needed his attention. He took a deep breath, counted to ten, and reminded himself he wasn't the only one putting in extra-long shifts. Kimberly had a lot on her plate with the sponsored corporate event, as well as an elderly grandparent she was taking care of.

She squeaked in dismay as the rings popped open, tipping the binder off her knees and onto the carpet, paper scattering across the floor in every direction. She jolted out of the chair, stumbling and knocking over a stack of paperwork on the edge of Wade's antique oak desk. It avalanched across the polished surface, toppling wooden picture frames and a crystal dish filled with butterscotch candies.

"Oh, Mr. Briggs, I'm so, so sorry." Kimberly bent to retrieve the papers.

A wave of frustration rolled through Wade as the muscles in his back knotted and began to throb. Kimberly was a hard worker who'd started out strong. In recent weeks, coinciding with her grandmother's health issues, she'd become klutzy and easily distracted. Her last catastrophe had resulted in an open water bottle spilling across her laptop keyboard, completely ruining the device. She'd misfiled reports, added meetings to his calendar for the wrong day, and scheduled an important meeting with Mr. Duncan Wright instead of Mr. Duncan White.

He stood to help, but Kimberly waved him off.

"I've got this. Just give me a minute."

"No problem." Wade accepted the framed photos of his sons, Kip and Luke, relieved the glass had not broken, and arranged them on the corner of his desk farthest away from

Kimberly, next to the sterling silver letter opener his mother had given him for Christmas.

He stared at the photos, transported momentarily, to happier times. When he came home from a long shift at the office and heard about the boys' day over family dinner. When his weekends were spent cheering them on from the sidelines at sporting events. When he and Juliet were a team, committed to each other and their sons. But that was then.

Damn it, he missed his boys. Juliet...well, he was still bitter about her betrayal but thankful to know the truth.

He straightened one of the frames and shifted his focus to the large oil painting on the wall, a gift from his mother when he was promoted to president of the company's North American division five years ago, while Kimberly gathered herself. The Wilhelm Brauer landscape represented one of the proudest days of his life. The warmth of accomplishment crept in as he remembered celebrating with everyone who mattered to him: his then-wife Juliet, his mother and three brothers, Roger, Gabe, and Phillip, and his sons.

Every furnishing he'd acquired to complete the classic décor in his office signified years of hard work, self-discipline, and sacrifice. A life's work, even though recent events had highlighted it could all disappear in a flash.

Thousands of livelihoods depended on his ability to save the North American division of Stallion Protection Partners. The burden felt like a cement block chained around his neck, and suddenly he needed some distance between everything his office represented and the corporate office's lack of commitment to its employees.

The message from headquarters in Australia was loud and clear: the bottom line was profit, not people.

Wade's boss, Stuart Flannigan, inherited a corporate leadership position because his father was chairman of the board. Sadly, that was the only factor that qualified him to serve as CEO. Flannigan put more effort into spending his millions and cycling through wives than optimizing the company's most valuable asset—people.

"Let's continue this meeting in the conference room. It might be easier to go over the paperwork if we can spread out." Wade collected the slew of folders stacked on the chair next to Kimberly and went into the meeting room adjacent to his office.

He stretched the muscles in his neck by rolling his head side-to-side, then lowered into a leather chair at the worktable, the room's casual décor inviting him to relax, get comfortable, and think outside the box. Wade spent a good portion of each day in this room, meeting with his leadership team and clients. Five years ago, he'd hired an interior decorator to remodel the space, replacing the dark paneling, long rectangular table, and old-fashioned chairs with a round glass-topped table, plush leather chairs, plants, and celery-colored textured wallpaper. The previous interior had been designed to impress and intimidate; the new interior created a work atmosphere that was warm and inviting and put everyone on a level playing field.

Too bad he couldn't get Flannigan to participate in a few team meetings. Maybe then he'd appreciate just how much talent the company stood to lose if even a single North American division was sold off.

Wade stretched his legs and crossed them at the ankle, happy for a moment of solitude.

Kimberly slunk into the conference room, the binder firmly held in both hands. "I'm really sorry, Mr. Briggs."

"Don't worry about it. Accidents happen." He couldn't resist peeking at his wristwatch, calculating the delay. His schedule was already backed up with meetings, consultations, and phone calls. That dedication and focus were two of the reasons he'd become the youngest executive officer to step into the role of division president. Would his talent and achievements be enough to save his employees? For that matter, would it be enough to preserve his own career?

"Here's the list you requested." Kimberly handed him a packet of paper, the first page now creased and wrinkled.

"Thanks." He scrutinized the list until he heard a muffled sniffle. He looked up to see tears coursing down his assistant's face. "Honestly, Kimberly, it's okay."

"It's just…with my grandma being so ill…" She looked up with red-rimmed eyes.

"Has she gotten worse? Do you need to stay home to help instead of going out to California?" His racing thoughts contradicted his sympathetic offer. "I'm sure there's someone in the company who can handle the event if you need to step away."

"No." She slumped in her chair. "I need to go, if for no other reason than to finish what I started. One of our neighbors volunteered to check on Grammy while I'm gone."

Wade leaned forward, elbows on the table. His impatience evaporated as he considered Kimberly's quandary, well acquainted with what it was like to be torn between competing obligations.

"Tell you what." He pushed a box of tissues across the table. "After this meeting, do whatever else you need to finish here, and then go home. Spend some time with your grandmother, make sure she has what she needs while you're gone, pack your bags, and get a good night's sleep."

"You're so kind, Mr. Briggs. I won't let you down." She patted her tears and offered a tremulous smile.

Uncomfortable with the gratitude shining on her face, he turned his attention to the activities list. He skimmed through the details, made a couple of notations, and handed it back. "I like how you arranged the information. It's easy to read and well organized. Send me a finalized copy and check that off your to-do list."

"I'll have to retype it." Kimberly fidgeted in embarrassment, her eyes again turning watery. "It was one of the files I lost when my computer crashed last week."

Wade counted to ten, barely holding onto his patience, but then reminded himself why he'd hired Kimberly in the first place. Top of her class, outstanding evaluations during her first year in the clerical pool, and a willingness to go over and above what was expected of her, until her grandmother became ill. His own work suffered during the divorce, but eventually he got back on track. Throwing himself into work to prevent any further decline and get his head back in the game had saved him—in more ways than one.

"Make a couple of copies, and we'll go with what we have," he said. "Let's just get through today and this event. Once we get back into the office, we'll talk to the IT department about getting you a better laptop and about you taking a few days off, so you can take care of your family."

"Thank you, but it's not necessary." Kimberly's eyes darkened with worry. "I don't need a new laptop. I've been very conscientious about purchasing supplies and when ordering business lunches to keep spending down. With the way the company is struggling, I'm surprised the annual award celebration is still happening."

"The company is not *struggling*, Kimberly." Wade's stomach muscles clenched, and he proceeded with caution. The last thing he wanted was employees panicking. "The North American division has been hit hard the last few quarters. Hurricanes in Louisiana and Florida caused a lot of damage, and we took a significant hit with all of the claims filed. That, coupled with the tornados in Oklahoma and wildfires in California, has resulted in higher than anticipated losses. It's standard procedure to evaluate operations when a company incurs financial losses. There might be restructuring, premium increases, a freeze on hiring...any number of strategies to protect the company's viability and profitability. I'm sure employees are starting to speculate about how Stallion plans to handle the impact, and some of them are worried about being downsized. Until an official statement is released from Corporate" —he glared at her sternly—"you *cannot* share what you know."

"I would never compromise the confidentiality my role as your assistant requires, Mr. Briggs." She stiffened in her seat, spine ramrod straight. "I don't engage in gossip or encourage speculation, but you should be aware that people are talking. More than that, they're worried."

Kimberly's statement indicated employees were picking up on signs of trouble. Part of the problem was Flannigan's refusal to bring North American leadership into the decision-making process. Wade often learned of developments after they occurred, such as Flannigan's meeting with their US competitor—and the logical option of selling off assets. It was a valid decision, but, in Wade's opinion, drastic action that could be avoided with strategic planning and careful management. As far as Wade could determine, Flannigan was still in negotiations and had not presented a final recommendation to the board.

Stallion was a for-profit conglomerate, but Wade had spent the past eight weeks running numbers and looking at alternatives to selling off or shutting down those units costing the corporation money. He just needed a face-to-face with Flannigan to convince the CEO his plan had merit. If Flannigan signed off on Wade's Hail Mary pass, hundreds of jobs would be saved.

Just thinking about the impacted families fueled Wade's determination to confront Flannigan and convince him not to downsize or offload any employees.

"I'm doing everything possible to avoid layoffs or closures." His tone was low, as if he was speaking more to himself than his assistant.

"You're a good leader, Mr. Briggs. People respect you." She closed the binder and pulled it to the table's edge. "I like the way you keep us informed. It makes me feel like I'm part of something bigger. I know we can trust you."

He cleared his throat to avoid responding to her statement. "Speaking of discretion, remember that one of the division winners will also be honored as the company-wide Employee of the Year. That announcement will be revealed at the actual award ceremony. Not a whisper to anyone."

"Of course." She nodded emphatically. "I reviewed the schedule yesterday, including the activities and amenities facilitated by the resort for the attendees, as well as company functions. The welcome reception is scheduled for the evening we arrive. I won't be able to relax until after the awards dinner. I want the home office in Australia to be totally impressed with our work."

Wade stroked the side of his temple as he sensed the beginnings of a headache. He tended to ignore the warning signs from his body telling him he needed to take a break. He'd take a few days off after convincing Flannigan not to chop jobs and after the company's top talent got the recognition they deserved.

"Are you feeling all right, Mr. Briggs? Would you like me to get you a glass of water? Should we adjourn the meeting?" Kimberly's brows furrowed in concern at his extended silence.

"No, we don't have much time." The best remedy for his stress was to confirm Kimberly hadn't overlooked any details. "Did you arrange for flowers and fruit baskets?"

"Yes." Kimberly handed him another list to add to the sheet of papers he already held.

"And the special gift for Sherry Kline?"

"I ordered the leather bound organizer with her initials on it, just as you asked." Kimberly studied him intently. "Gosh, wouldn't that be awful? To be named corporate Employee of the Year and then lose your job? Too bad she's employed by the office with the biggest losses."

And the most attractive purchase option, he thought. Wade's carotid vein throbbed in his neck as he thought about Kimberly's comment.

What would he do if Sherry Kline confronted him about a potential buyout that included the Iowa unit? If she, or any other employee, straight out asked, morally and ethically he felt obligated to tell the truth. But honesty could jeopardize his career and a potential sale, not to mention the chaos it would generate among the workforce. Flannigan was stingy with factual information, but he'd made it clear his utmost priority was the bottom line. As president of the North American division, Wade and other top-level leaders were under a non-disclosure order about a potential sale that included several poor-performing offices, Iowa included

The only reason Kimberly was aware jobs were on the line was because she'd been taking notes during the video call when Stuart Flannigan bragged about negotiating a ridiculously low price with a domestic insurance company. Laughing at how cleverly he'd countered what Wade knew to be a fair offer, Flannigan was already patting himself on the back for giving stockholders a fine profit. Still, the decision wasn't final until approved by the board, and most of them were smart enough to appreciate the long-term potential of holding onto assets instead of selling them off to make a fast buck.

"Let me finish this." Wade studied the report closer than necessary, intentionally not acknowledging his assistant's comment. All he needed was for her to slip and mention something that would jeopardize his plans to convince Flannigan to at least hold off on selling any units until he'd had a chance to prove the company was better off hanging onto them.

Kimberly reviewed her copy of the list. "The Silver Fox Resort looks like a great place to hold this event. I've been working with Amy Denham to coordinate things from our side. The Fosters, who own the place, have done a good job accommodating our needs."

Ah, yes, the Silver Fox Resort. Wade's mouth went dry as pain filled his heart. He struggled with the memory which forced its way into his mind.

He'd been to the resort before, and even though it had still been under construction, the place was amazing. He'd immediately been drawn to the beach and gardens and hiking trails and vineyard.

He understood why Flannigan chose this particular venue for the corporate event—his new wife had suggested it and Flannigan agreed to keep her happy, according to the corporate grapevine. The resort was ideal, but Wade struggled with the thought of returning. He didn't want to be reminded of his last visit.

He'd taken Juliet to the resort for their wedding anniversary three years earlier. The once-beautiful memories —the wedding, their marriage, and the second honeymoon— were now tainted by her infidelity.

"Never thought I'd be headed back there," he muttered under his breath.

"The Silver Fox Resort is one of the top-rated resorts in California. Is there a problem?" Kimberly's brows furrowed.

"No. No problem. Everything looks perfect." He forced a smile. His feelings about the resort didn't matter. The award winners would love it. "Anything else or are we done?"

With a quick nod to indicate they'd covered everything,

Kimberly gathered up the binders and folders. "I'll be in the office a few more hours, and then I'll head out. You can reach me on my cell if you need anything."

Elbows on the armrests of his chair, Wade steepled his fingers. His eyes closed wearily, his mind idly reviewing the conversation and bringing the image of Sherry Kline to mind. Her earnest features were imprinted on his memory from their most recent video call.

A burst of pride expanded in his chest. He was pleased this year's corporate Employee of the Year was one of the best project managers he'd ever worked with. It added credence to his argument that retaining top talent was the smarter strategic decision.

Sherry was a dedicated, hardworking employee who generously shared her talents to benefit the company. In exchange for that dedication, her job was on the line, one of many that hung in the balance between profit and performance. That irony eroded his pride like acid.

He *had to* convince Flannigan that preserving jobs and retaining loyal employees was more valuable than a one-time sale. While everyone else was enjoying the amenities of the Silver Fox Resort, Wade would be negotiating the biggest deal of his career. He hoped the outcome of his professional relationship fared better than his marriage.

The last thing he wanted was to walk away from the beauty of the California coast with the weight of another failure on his shoulders.

Chapter 3

Sherry wiped her sweaty palms on her navy skirt as the airplane wheels touched ground at San Francisco International Airport. Emily, a chatty grandmother-type in the seat next to her, patted her arm as she started to gather her jacket and tote bag.

"Have fun this week, dear," the friendly woman said with a smile.

Sherry's stomach pitched as the plane slowed and eased up to the gate.

Making her way toward the luggage carousel, she slowed behind an elderly couple. The woman let out a little yawn and leaned against the man. He curved his hand around her waist and kissed the woman's temple.

She missed those small, inconsequential gestures. With John gone, she no longer had that intimacy, the silent language that developed when a man and woman spent years together.

Entirely fixated on the interaction, she almost missed her luggage. By the time she reached for her second checked bag, impatient passengers were jostling for a place along the carousel. She backed away, looked around for the arrival zone signs, and then headed for the escalator to find her ride.

Car exhaust, honking horns, and people talking washed over her as she made her way toward the parking structure. Reaching the sidewalk, she spotted a broad-shouldered man holding a sign with her name written in bold block letters. The brawny, chestnut-haired driver looked to be in his early thirties. He wore black trousers and a gold shirt embroidered with the Silver Fox Resort logo.

"Hello." She waved to flag his attention. "I'm Sherry Kline."

"Welcome to California, ma'am." His deep, masculine voice was warm and friendly. "I'm Alex. May I take your luggage for you?"

"Yes, please." She waited while Alex loaded her suitcases into the large minibus. Her face heated as he hefted the largest bag. She reached for her carry-on as he lifted the second suitcase. "It looks like I over-packed."

"Better to over-pack than leave something important at home. That's what my wife tells me." He gestured to the open door. "Why don't you go ahead and get seated? We'll be ready to take off in just a moment."

All around her, the other passengers and their family or friends seemed to be in a joyous mood. Sherry spotted a couple embracing as they shared a kiss. From the woman's attire, she'd just arrived home from a business trip. Sherry looked longingly at the couple, remembering when she used to meet John at the arrival terminal in Des Moines. Having driven herself to the airport that morning and parked her car in the long-term lot, there'd be no one to greet her when she returned home. Her heart squeezed when the man gently lifted the woman off her feet for a final hurrah kiss. The love they shared pinched her with a sting of envy.

Once upon a time, John had looked at Sherry like the

traveler looked at her partner. Guilt for taking those looks for granted pressed in.

She smiled sadly as she continued to watch the people around her, hoping they realized how lucky they were. Not everyone found true love, but she had. What was that poem about 'twas better to have loved and lost than never to have loved at all? Easy to say until the one you loved was gone.

Shaking her head, she reminded herself she needed to keep the past firmly where it belonged—in the past—and focus only on the future. This vacation was an important milestone in her new life. Overcoming her trepidation about making the trip was an achievement to be proud of. At least, that's what she'd been telling herself.

"Would you like to get into the van, ma'am?" Alex stood next to the front of the shuttle, hands crossed in front of him.

"What? Oh, yes." She tugged her purse higher on her shoulder.

The wind gently tossed the hem of her skirt as she walked toward the levered door of the silver and blue minibus. As she climbed up the short stairwell, she noted a coffee maker and micro-fridge, indicating this was not going to be an ordinary shuttle ride. Inside the thirteen-seat bus, Sherry caught sight of another passenger. The attractive older man leaned back in one of the padded leather seats, head bent over the tablet in one hand as he tapped the screen.

It took a few seconds to register that the athletic silver fox in khakis and a royal blue golf shirt was Wade Briggs, the guy in charge of Stallion's North American operations.

She was accustomed to seeing him in a suit and tie, well-groomed, friendly and approachable, capable and decisive. Today, he was even more charismatic than he came across on video or telephone. She took advantage of the opportunity to check him out up close and in person.

A scan of his face revealed a slightly crooked nose she

suspected had been broken once, maybe twice. Salt and pepper hair had never appealed to her, but on him, the gray and almost white sides looked handsome and distinguished.

She wondered about a wife, but a quick peek at his left hand was telling. Like her, he appeared to be traveling alone.

Wade lifted his head, his casual glance shifting to recognition. For those brief seconds, she wondered what he saw because the flare of interest wasn't that of boss and employee but that of a man appreciating a woman.

Her automatic smile froze in place. His open appraisal triggered a flurry of unexpected emotions—pleasure, panic, guilt. She forced her lips to curve upwards, masking her uncertainty. When he continued to assess her, she pretended to admire the luxurious fittings: the overhead lighting, black upholstery, gray carpet runner.

"Hello, Sherry. I see you made it here on time." Wade smiled, revealing straight, pearl-white teeth.

"Hi, Mr. Briggs." She sounded like a breathless teenager encountering her favorite movie star. "Yes, the flight was on time."

"Please. Call me Wade." He nodded to a nearby seat. "We'll all be on a first-name basis by tonight."

With a breath locked in her lungs, she couldn't speak. She'd prepared herself for banter and casual conversation with her coworkers, but not the executives. Plus, she'd not once considered any kind of physical attraction, yet her whole body was lighting up and tingling with one look from Wade.

"Sit here." He pointed to the seat across from him. "We can chat on the way up about your current project, or if you prefer, we don't have to talk business at all. It's not every day I get to chat with the star."

"The star?" Sherry fought to hear what the man was saying over her pounding heart. "What do you mean?"

"I'm teasing you, but you *are* the star of the Des Moines office." He thumbed off his tablet and tucked it into a leather satchel on the seat next to him.

"I am?" She felt the polarized pull of modesty and pride. Sure, she'd been voted the Des Moines office Employee of the Year, but there were many other deserving employees. It took each person contributing to the team for them to succeed together.

"Yes, you are. Your diligence and the way you pay attention to detail amazes me." He unbuckled his seatbelt and lifted the armrest. "Here, let me stow your jacket and carry-on." His muscles rippled beneath his shirt as he lifted the bag to an overhead rack. "According to our driver, it's an hour and a half journey to the resort."

Oh, sweet heavens. What are we going to talk about?

"Thank you. I don't mean to be a bother." She slid a glance at his flat abdomen and strong thighs, wondering what Alison would think of him.

"You're never a bother, Sherry."

She sat, pulling her skirt down self-consciously, then she stretched her legs under the seat in front. The extra room did nothing to relieve the ache in her joints.

"Are you comfortable?" he asked in a gentle tone.

She nodded, lowering her gaze. It had been three years since a man so solicitously looked after her. The concern warmed her but also discomfited her.

"Looks like it will be just you two." Alex climbed the stairs and stood at the head of the aisle, steadying himself on the silver metal bar that ran overhead. "The other flight we were waiting on has been delayed."

"I don't mind waiting." It was second nature for Sherry to accommodate others' needs, and in this case, she desperately wanted the presence of others to distract Wade Briggs's keen attention.

Sherry and Wade had communicated several times about work projects, but she didn't know anything about him. She'd never been good at small talk. John had always taken the lead on those conversations. Now, she faced ninety, long minutes alone with her attractive boss.

She reached into her purse, grabbed a paperback book, and opened to a random page, hoping Wade would get the hint and not try to engage her in chit-chat.

"Have you been to Sonoma Valley before?" he asked as he settled back in his seat.

Oh, this portion of the trip was not heading in the direction she had hoped. She hadn't been to California or New York or even Florida. They'd always planned to travel after John retired, arrogantly assuming they had plenty of time. She didn't feel that way anymore. She'd learned the hard way that each second counted.

"No, I haven't traveled much, but I think this trip is going to be a nice change of pace."

Wade leaned forward as if sharing a secret. "You know? I think you're right."

Chapter 4

*W*ade took in Sherry like he was drinking in a tall glass of water. He enjoyed how she kept looking at him out of the corner of her eye. The tentativeness was a contrast to her professional persona. In project meetings, she was in control and confident in proposing innovative problem-solving ideas. During the last brainstorming session, she'd come up with several money-saving solutions that piggybacked off his own strategies.

So caught up in his thoughts of her, Wade barely noticed Alex thumbing notes onto his phone—checking in with the resort, he assumed. Once finished, the driver offered each of them a bottled water labeled with the resort's logo.

"We'll reach the Silver Fox Resort in an hour and forty minutes if traffic is good today," Alex said. Cocking his head, he gazed curiously at Wade. "Have you stayed with us before, sir?"

"Yes." Impressed, he noted Alex appeared to have filled out since the last time he saw him. Three years ago, the driver's six-foot frame had bordered on scrawny.

"I thought I recognized you, but I wasn't sure until I got a second look. You were here, what, two years ago?"

"Close enough." The reference to his last visit brought up unpleasant memories which threatened to ruin his good mood. "It's nice to see you again. As I recall, you waited quite a while when my flight had to be rerouted because of weather issues."

Three years ago, he'd come to the coast for his wedding anniversary. The resort wasn't open then as the finishing touches and operating procedures were being finalized, but he'd gotten acquainted with the Foster siblings when they needed insurance coverage for their business and were accepting bids. He'd immediately been impressed with the resort's potential for success.

"Flights into San Francisco are often delayed," Alex explained. "We try to avoid inconveniencing our guests, so flexibility is part of the job."

"How's your mom? Did she pull through her brain surgery?"

"You remember that?" Alex's brown eyes widened in surprise. "She's fine. If I remember correctly, you told me to stay strong for her and to not give up hope. The doctors were worried she wasn't going to make it, but we got our miracle."

"It never hurts to believe. Sometimes that conviction is what others need to endure a difficult situation." Wade caught Sherry following the conversation from the corner of his eye and wondered what she was making of the exchange.

"Her recovery wasn't the only miracle. Mom's surgery was thousands of dollars, even with insurance. The hospital wouldn't schedule it until we had a large enough down payment. The next time I took Mom in for a checkup, the doctor gave me a date for the procedure. He said an anonymous donor had agreed to cover the out-of-pocket expenses." Alex's eyes drilled into his. "You wouldn't know anything about how those bills got paid, would you?"

Wade thought back to the phone call he'd overheard and Alex's desperate promise to pay the five-thousand-dollar deductible. He'd told whoever was on the phone his mother didn't have much time and a delay could cost her her life.

A few discreet inquiries at the resort enabled Wade to do what needed to be done. He had the money needed to save a woman's life. An anonymous payment to the hospital and the crisis was resolved. Wade had fixed it, like he always fixed problems.

"Why would you think I'd know anything about that?" Wade's chest tightened, but he kept his expression relaxed.

"Timing, maybe? We got the good news right after I met you. You caught me at a low spot in my life, and I over-shared, dumping all my worries on you, including the financial crisis delaying her surgery. I can count how many people knew about our financial situation on one hand." Alex's gaze bored into him, then he shrugged. "Maybe you're just good luck. We still don't know who paid the deductible, but we are forever indebted to the person." Alex turned to lock the security brackets on the coffee maker and refrigerator door. "Mom's got a part-time job at the grocery store in town. Doctor says she might live to be a hundred."

Wade let out a stifled breath. "That's wonderful. I'm happy for your family."

At twenty, Wade had taken on responsibility for his mother and younger brothers when their father died unexpectedly. He understood what it was like to be accountable, and he took protecting his family seriously.

Alex situated himself behind the steering wheel and turned on the engine.

Sherry looked at him with an impish smile. "Did you know your eyebrows go up when you're telling a fib?"

A surge of heat expanded from his chest upward. "Interesting." He looked away, unable to control the nervous tapping of his toe. He wondered if Sherry would pick up on that tell, startled to realize he didn't mind her eyes on him.

He thrived on helping friends, family, employees, even strangers. Helping others was as natural to him as breathing. Now, he was responsible for thousands of employees. He'd never get tired of being a solid anchor for the people he cared about. He'd learned early on life wasn't fair. Bad things happened to good people. Honest, hardworking, decent people. He couldn't control fate and he couldn't solve problems for everyone, but a single small act of kindness could make a huge difference for someone facing difficulties. Experiencing the compassion and kindness of teachers, neighbors, and community members had taught him that when his father died, leaving their family in a dire financial situation.

That thought reminded him unpleasantly of his mission to convince Flannigan it was better in the long run to save jobs instead of selling off those units hit by heavy losses. He shoved the concern away. There was plenty of time for worry. For now, he wanted to enjoy the interlude with Sherry Kline.

"So, what are you reading?" Wade motioned to the paperback on her lap.

She picked up the book and offered the spine so he could read the title. "A novel my neighbor recommended."

Ah, yes. The goodness of neighbors.

"It's about a British woman who falls in love with a German soldier during World War II." She summarized the few chapters she'd read so far.

"A romantic book then." He made note of the fact Sherry enjoyed reading.

"And history. I like the combination of the two. If a book

doesn't have enough of both, I tend to lose interest. My husband used to tease me about leaving half-finished books throughout the house." She shifted on her seat, the bright smile fading as if the memory saddened her. She turned her face toward the window, a faint blush staining her cheeks.

Wade pondered her reaction. Sherry seemed embarrassed, perhaps for sharing intimate personal details. He realized how little he knew about her, aside from her professional credentials and the stellar work she'd accomplished for the Des Moines office. He did recall hearing she'd rejoined the workforce after her husband died unexpectedly.

Losing a spouse created all kinds of deaths. The death of a marriage, the death of dreams, the death of trust and love. Then again, he'd experienced his own kind of death with divorce. He'd grieved when he and Juliet separated. His love and faith in her had been wiped away by her betrayal. Sherry's anguish at losing a husband she loved must have been even more devastating.

He never expected to be a midlife bachelor and had zero interest in the dating scene, but there were times he longed for the comfort and companionship of a committed relationship. He wondered how Sherry had adjusted to life as a widow. Had she formed friendships with other single women her age—the types who signed up for cruises and clubs and outings as a group? Was she a doting grandmother who filled her evenings and weekends with chubby-cheeked toddlers? Or did she sit in a silent house, reading historical romance books?

With her gaze pinned on the passing landscape, Wade studied Sherry. Mid-to-late forties, wavy shoulder-length blond-brown hair pulled back in a simple black hair clip, minimal makeup that gave her wholesome charm, sensible flats, and a tailored skirt with a matching light blue sweater.

At first glance, she looked like any other Midwestern mom and wife. Grounded, practical, responsible. A trim figure maintained through portion control and daily walks, maybe with the family dog—a cocker spaniel or some other friendly, not-too-large breed. She seemed the type to volunteer at her kids' school or serve as the team mom for soccer or little league baseball. He wondered about kids—did she have any and were they grown or maybe still teenagers living at home?

Sherry Kline was the kind of woman single guys his age might overlook. Single guys he knew wanted someone unencumbered by responsibilities like motherhood and caregiver so she could feed their egos and cater to their needs and wants. However, Sherry was exactly the kind of woman who would appeal to him...if he was in the market for a relationship. With her wide, curious blue eyes, team-player attitude, diligent work ethic, and soft curves, she seemed the type who valued home and family and commitment.

He gave a mental shake.

Sherry exuded a natural warmth and concern for others that made him want to tell Alex to take the scenic route to the resort so that he had her all to himself for a while longer. He hadn't felt the pull of attraction like this in years, but employees were off-limits. Period. The risk of a sexual harassment lawsuit should a relationship not work out was all too real. Maintaining clear personal boundaries meant neither he nor an employee was put into a potentially uncomfortable position.

He pulled his eyes away from Sherry's profile and fumbled for a neutral topic to continue the conversation. *Books.* Books were safe.

"I like to read biographies myself." His voice sounded loud above the rumble of the shuttle's engine, and he cleared his throat self-consciously at her startled glance. "I usually discover something about the person I never would have guessed about them. People are always a surprise. You think you know someone well, and then…"

Juliet had proven that point numerous times.

"On one of our team calls, you mentioned a book about a Navy SEAL you were reading. You said it wasn't a leadership book as much as a memoir." She relaxed into her seat. "I ordered it for my son. He's twenty-five and an avid reader. He liked having me to read to him when he was young. It was the perfect excuse to take a break from laundry or dusting."

"Books always make nice holiday or birthday gifts," he murmured, remembering how Juliet had been too impatient to sit and read to Kip and Luke.

"Oh, the book wasn't a present." She raised her brows, as if puzzled. "I pick up stuff for my kids all the time. Whenever I see something I know they need or might appreciate."

On top of Sherry's already impressive list of qualities, he added kindness. His mother had been thoughtful like that. Getting up early on her days off to make banana pancakes for him and his brothers. Giving up a Saturday afternoon to drive him and his buddies to the movies before he had a driver's license. Doing his household chores during finals so he could study.

His mom and Sherry would get along well, unlike his ex-wife.

Juliet was a drama queen who argued with everyone and turned family gatherings into horror shows. Sherry seemed the type who'd offer to help with dishes and who would show up with the perfect hostess gift.

He'd wandered off into his own thoughts again, an awkward silence stretching between them.

"I'll let you get back to whatever you were doing." She reached into her bag and pulled out a set of earphones.

"Sorry," he apologized with a rueful smile. "I'm usually a better conversationalist. You remind me...I mean, I feel very at ease with you even though I hardly know you. We're both about the same age. Single. Career-oriented. You have kids. I have kids. They're probably relatively close in age, young people as opposed to toddlers, right? It's nice to talk to someone who's on the same page." He sucked in a quick breath, deciding now was a good time to clarify boundaries. "It's *very* nice to enjoy a mature conversation with a woman who isn't scoping me out for a wedding band and net worth."

She giggled, the sound sweet and husky at the same time, as if they were sharing a private joke.

"I can see where that would get old," she said.

He thought back over what he just said and rolled his eyes. "Sheesh, I sound very full of myself, don't I? I just meant—"

"No explanation required," she assured him. "Rich, my older brother, recently divorced and has become a serial playboy. Fifty years old, driving a bright-red Corvette, dating women younger than my daughter. He has a new girlfriend every month. I never knew there were that many twentysomethings willing to settle for a paunchy, balding, middle-aged man so long as he bankrolls their designer handbags and acrylic nails." She nodded toward him. "You're physically fit and have all your hair. That's icing on the cake for girls looking for a sugar daddy."

He burst out laughing. Her colorful description held a hint of snark he never would have expected from someone as prim and professional as she conducted herself in the work setting. Not for the first time, he suspected there were intriguing layers beneath her polished, proficient façade.

"I promise I won't drift off again if you care to continue our chat." He folded his arms and slouched to get comfortable, extending his legs and crossing his ankles.

She hesitated and slid the earphone case back in her bag. The way her eyes flicked to him spoke again of her nervousness. He would need to remedy that uneasiness.

"What were you going to listen to?" he asked, eager to learn more about her. Were their tastes in music similar? What hobbies did she enjoy? Did she like to dine out or cook at home?

"Oh, just some background noise. Rain. Waves rolling onto the shore. Nature." She tucked her book away also. "I have a variety of soundtracks that help me block out noise and focus. Like you, my mind sometimes wanders, even when I'm in the middle of something."

"Does your daughter like to read, as well?" he asked.

"She's more into audiobooks. She listens to everything from romance to self-help books to thrillers." A fleeting expression of sadness crossed her face and then disappeared. "My husband was the same way. Alison takes after him in looks and temperament."

She must have caught him glancing at her left hand because she rubbed the finger where her wedding band would have been.

"If you are wondering, my husband's been gone three years." Her throat spasmed, but she remained composed.

"My mom was a young widow like you," he said. "My dad was killed in a car accident when I was twenty. I still had brothers at home." His mom had toughed it out for her kids, juggling the roles of breadwinner, head of household, and single parent with grace, tenacity, and humor. He imagined Sherry's experience much the same. He'd helped as much as he could, keeping his brothers on the straight and narrow and putting himself through college with the support and encouragement of a generous mentor he still met for lunch once a month.

"I never thought I'd be a widow at forty-six," she

admitted. "John and I were just starting to plan for retirement. Tyler was in his final year of college when John died, and Alison was a college sophomore. They both wanted to drop out to stay home with me, but I refused to let that be an option." Her eyes got misty. "I'd been a stay-at-home mom for years, but I needed a job, so all three of us got lost in our studies. I'm so fortunate to have found this job."

His mouth became dry and he tried to swallow his uneasiness. "We're lucky to have gained such a talented project manager." He frowned. "I'm just sorry it was because you were forced to find a job. Entering the workplace again, after so many years, must have been hard."

"Thank you for not avoiding the topic." Her voice was soft. "So many people avoid talking about death and loss. I've even lost touch with several of our old friends because they're uncomfortable talking about John's death and the changes that came with losing him."

Again, Wade was struck by a sense of camaraderie with Sherry. He'd lost friends after the divorce. Become isolated. Threw himself into work and taking care of his employees because he'd lost everything else that mattered.

"Maybe we should stick to the weather. I'm sure you don't want to hear my sad story." Sherry knotted her fingers together. "I'm not very adept at small talk. John said that was why we were such a perfect pair. He talked, and I listened."

"Maybe it's me, not you. I work a lot. Maybe I'm out of practice talking about personal stuff."

Three years. It had been three years since his divorce. The same length of time since Sherry had lost her husband.

Was Sherry still in love, even though her husband was gone? Had she resumed dating? Some nice corporate guy who took her out to dinner Saturday night and stayed over for Sunday brunch? The thought bothered him more than it should.

"My mom was a straight shooter who liked to talk," he said. "Raising four sons, she learned how to draw out information and listen. No topic was off-limits, no matter how tough."

Sherry's hand went to her throat, fingers fluttering nervously, giving him the impression she'd had enough candid conversation. He reminded himself they were on a corporate vacation, not the Dr. Phil show. No need for further self-analysis or exchanging deep, dark secrets.

"I think you might be right. We should stick to the weather." He winked, hoping to get her to relax. "The California coast is famous for its moody climate. Cold and foggy in the morning. Sunny and warm in the afternoon." He ignored the pang of disappointment at the mundane turn of topic. "I never asked—did you find the material we sent for your trip satisfactory?"

He leaned back against the leather headrest to get a better view of her pretty eyes, the blue reminding him of a tropical sea. A few unruly curls had escaped her clip, drawing his attention to the soft skin at her temples. Tiny silver earrings nestled in her earlobes. He could happily inventory her features all day.

"Kimberly did an exceptional job putting the information together." Her eyes brightened. "To be honest, all of the options are a bit overwhelming. Yoga. Pottery. Wine tasting. It was hard to choose."

Her smooth voice was like listening to a forest brook, a melodic rise and fall of tone and emotion soothing and invigorating at the same time.

"What activities did you decide on? Yoga or pottery?" he guessed.

"Just the session on painting, actually. Wine and canvas parties are quite popular in Des Moines. Yoga is a little too exotic for me, although my daughter loves Zumba. Kimberly said I could add more activities to my itinerary after arriving at the resort and learning more." She sat up, excitement sharpening her features as she gazed into the distance. "Is that the Golden Gate Bridge?"

Her reaction deepened his curiosity. "In another ten minutes or so, we should be driving over it."

"I've always wanted to see the bridge. I hear the view is spectacular."

"Yes. It's beautiful." Funny, but he wasn't thinking of the bridge just then. Unable to resist, he said, "I'd like to hear more about your kids if you want to share."

Sherry turned her attention back to him, her face lighting up and blossoming into a wide, genuine smile. The freckles across her nose added fresh-faced appeal. "Are you asking to be polite, or are you really curious?"

Her proud mama-bear attitude made him sad his own sons hadn't experienced that kind of maternal devotion.

He nodded encouragement.

"My daughter is interning at a local bank in the home loan department." Sherry's mouth curved up into shallow dimples, conveying she was crazy about her children and proud of their accomplishments. "She's waiting for her boyfriend, Derrick, to graduate with his master's in business administration from Drake University. Once he gets a job offer, they'll probably move in together."

"Drake is a great school. I've given a couple of lectures there. They've got a nice setup." Wade pointed out the window. "There's your Golden Gate Bridge." He didn't mean to interrupt the easy conversation but didn't want her to miss the sight she'd looked forward to seeing.

Passing over the bridge allowed him time to admire her without any awkwardness. He relished her childlike wonder, her thrill and appreciation for small pleasures. The tiny flashes of the real, unguarded Sherry confirmed his suspicion she was a complex, dynamic woman.

"It's the most beautiful bridge I've ever seen." Her voice rang with awe.

"Yes, it is." He said no more, allowing her to fill her senses with the magnitude of the structure spanning the entrance to San Francisco Bay.

On the other side of the bridge, she turned back to him, interest glimmering in her eyes. "I didn't know you lectured at the university. What do you think of Iowa?"

"It's nice. Flat, but nice." He chuckled. "Then again, I can't imagine living anywhere but Denver. I've lived in Colorado most of my life."

"I've heard the Rocky Mountains are beautiful. I've never been there. Hopefully, I'll get to visit someday."

Now, there was an idea. Maybe he could invite her to Denver on the pretext of a job offer at the North American division offices. She was one of the company's strongest performers and continued to demonstrate her dedication and problem-solving abilities. Employee success and achievement were clear indicators of strong leadership, and one of the benchmarks he measured himself against every day.

Stuart Flannigan had no idea of the potential loss a decision to sell off units could cost Stallion Protection Partners. There were a hundred ways to generate revenue, but not half as many methods to recruit and retain loyal team members.

He rubbed two fingers over his temple, feeling the start of a stress headache.

"Do you have kids, Mr. Briggs?"

"Call me Wade, please."

"Okay, Wade, do you have kids?" She said his name like

she was testing it out, rolling the vowels and consonants over her tongue to savor the taste.

What was he doing?

It felt very much like flirting.

The casual banter of a man and woman getting acquainted over coffee or drinks. The playful but deliberate back and forth designed to ferret out details as to the other's suitability as a potential companion, partner, lover.

He'd be better off sticking to a discussion about weather and iconic landmarks, but he couldn't resist learning more about Sherry. He genuinely liked and admired her. There was nothing wrong with that. Right?

But he was self-aware enough to recognize the potential for trouble. He hadn't experienced these intense sensations for a long time—the playful push and pull of conversation, testing parameters, gauging reactions, and reading between the lines. It was nothing more than a friendly conversation because Sherry was a company employee. Still, the bus was their private bubble, and he was going to enjoy the moment.

"I have two sons. Luke and Kip. Both will be attending the University of Colorado, Boulder, in September. Before you ask, they aren't twins. They're ten months apart in age, which put them in the same grade when they started school."

"Are they following in your footsteps? Majoring in business or some other area of study?" Admiration lent a warm shine to her eyes so that they glimmered like gemstones. "If you're like me, there's no comparing pride in our kids' accomplishments to our own."

Of everything the divorce cost him, seeing the boys on a daily basis was the greatest loss. Juliet had moved out of state before filing for divorce, turning custody into a horrible battle. Ultimately, he quit fighting her to spare the boys from additional turmoil. Teenagers at the time, they'd been more focused on sports and girls and skateboarding than splitting time between Denver and Boston.

Wade was ecstatic when they both chose to attend the University of Colorado and thanked fate for the opportunity to rebuild the close bond they'd shared before the divorce.

"I've always been proud of my sons. Both were accepted into the School of Engineering. I'm happy they're at school together. They're always trying to outdo each other. It's been that way since they were toddlers." Pain tightened in a band around his heart. "Being together will keep them focused. They're super competitive so we steered them into different sports. Kip plays baseball, and Luke is into soccer."

"You don't strike me as competitive," Sherry mused, studying his face. "Ambitious, yes. Competitive, no. Is that a trait they inherited from their mother?"

"Juliet hasn't worked a day in her life." The pleasure in his gut soured. "Sorry, I don't mean to speak ill of my ex-wife, but it's the truth. Kip and Luke take after my father. He was clever and charismatic. Always wanted to be the best, do the best, achieve the most. He was a good provider, but we weren't always his top priority. Still, I'm sorry the boys never had an opportunity to know him."

"Losing John so suddenly, like you lost your father, taught me the importance of doing things now instead of waiting." A shadow darkened her eyes, and she whispered, "Tomorrow is promised to no one."

Oh, wasn't that the truth. He'd thought the company was solid. Assumed every job was secure and would remain so. He still hoped to find an alternative to the proposed selloffs, but time was running out. If he didn't persuade Flannigan of the merits of an alternative solution, he'd be responsible for the failure.

If he failed his employees, each with a story like Sherry and each who was a valuable asset, it would be a repeat of his failure as a father. He'd assumed his marriage was rock-solid. Assumed he and Juliet would be life partners, grow old together, and share the joy of watching their sons mature into fine young men. He took that solidity for granted, and it cost him big.

Sherry picked up the thread of conversation, chatting about her son, activities she and her kids enjoyed together, and revealing her passion for creating organic body care products.

Wade realized he'd accomplished at least one mission—getting Sherry to relax and let down her guard. That was a small win compared to the monstrous challenge confronting him—saving employees' jobs—but he'd happily take it.

Chapter 5

$\mathcal{A}$s the shuttle's door eased open with a wheeze, Sherry's stomach fluttered with excitement as Wade reached for her hand to help her out of her seat. The gesture was unexpected, and unnecessary, but she took his hand anyway.

Her toes curled inside her flats as the surge of pleasure inside her heightened. Senses whirling with the woodsy scent of his cologne and the smooth warmth of his skin on hers, she wondered how it would feel to lean into his arms and inhale a lungful of his irresistible masculine scent. She released his hand before she did something impulsive, reminding herself this was her *boss*.

She accepted her jacket from Wade and quickly exited the bus to regain her bearings. The stunning scenery and salty ocean breeze helped. The sky was a work of art. Her eyes wandered over the stretch of rolling hills and the tall trees surrounding the resort. Her heart lifted momentarily as her fear of attending the event alone faded...because clearly Wade was solo like she was.

He paused behind her, his unique scent wrapping around

her like a comfortable hug. She gave in to the serenity of the location, her mind immediately wandering to thoughts of a men's line of soap and bath products. She could introduce a few new products at one of the upcoming craft fairs she'd signed up to attend. She inhaled, memorizing the combination of pine and earth and ocean.

The resort was every bit as impressive as the natural landscape. Situated on more than four hundred acres, the complex included the main building, private villas and cottages, retreat buildings, a stable, a vineyard, a pool and fitness center, and an assortment of other amenities. The rustic wood and stone construction blended into the natural beauty of the setting but promised a luxurious escape.

"I love the ocean." Sherry inhaled the salty ocean air. "Seeing the white caps reminds me of the summer John and I took our kids to Big Creek State Park. There's nothing better than the cool lake breeze sweeping across your skin. It always does wonders for the soul. The sound of the water lapping against the shore is like a soothing melody. I bet the waves crashing on the beach is even better." She grimaced when she realized she was letting her excitement get the better of her. When she fixed her eyes on Wade, there was no annoyance but an inexplicable sadness, which drew her concern.

She began to reach for him but jerked her hand away. *What was she thinking?* The intimate ride from the airport had blurred the boundaries between personal and professional. A line she must reestablish immediately.

Wade was easy to talk to and they seemed to have had some similar experiences that created common ground, but that didn't give her the right to behave so familiarly with a company executive.

She shrugged into her jacket to disguise the impulsive

gesture. "Wade? You mentioned you've been here before. You don't seem pleased to be here again. Is everything okay?"

"I'm fine." His smile was stiff, artfully disguising his feelings.

"Your whole demeanor shifted when you stepped off the shuttle." She hesitated. "I don't mean to pry. I'm a project manager. It's my nature to want to fix things."

"And that's what makes you excel at your job." His mouth relaxed into an approving curve. "As you apparently garnered from my conversation with Alex, I've been here before. This place carries some unpleasant memories. But like you said, this visit is going to be a nice change of pace."

"I've never been on a vacation without my husband and kids." She took a deep breath. "This is all new to me, and a bit overwhelming."

Like a rock shattering a glass window, the spell holding her back was broken. Her fears and insecurities seemed childish.

"Wouldn't it be nice to erase the past and go forward without painful memories and regrets shackling every step?" He spoke just above a whisper.

The words, so close to her own thoughts, made her shiver.

"I want to feel like I'm visiting for the first time," he confided. "The beauty of Silver Fox Resort is amazing, and I don't want this stay tarnished by the past."

"It's not easy to let go of the emotional baggage we carry. Each experience shapes us and leaves its mark," Sherry murmured. "But this place does seem magical. It's like stepping into another world where anything is possible."

A throbbing desire to walk on the beach, hand-in-hand with someone special, as the sun set over the ocean unsettled her. She stepped away from Wade so she didn't do something ridiculous like slip her hand into his. In her haste, she backed into the stack of suitcases Alex had pulled off the shuttle. A small cry rolled out of her mouth as she struggled to maintain her balance. Wade snaked his arm around her waist to steady her, bringing their bodies into contact. Her heart quickened as heat flared up her neck and her cheeks burned with embarrassment.

"Are you okay?" he asked, slowly pulling his arm away.

"Yes, thanks to your quick reflexes. Landing on my fanny in the parking lot isn't the grand entrance I imagined." She straightened her clothing and squared her shoulders. "I'm more embarrassed than anything. I need to be more careful."

His befuddled expression matched her own reaction to the brief press of his body against hers. He'd only touched her for a few seconds, yet a swell of emotion filled her— sweet relief at finding herself safe in his protective embrace with an electrifying undercurrent of sexual attraction.

It was the latter reaction that prompted a soft gasp.

Alison had gently broached the topic of dating, but Sherry insisted she wasn't ready. She'd lost the love of her life. No one could replace John. Even thinking about another man *in that way* made her feel guilty. Why, of all people, was she suddenly attracted to the CEO of her company?

Stunned, she realized Wade was speaking.

"I hope you get to meet Zoey Foster. She and her family own this place, but I think it's her vision that creates the magic. I can't wait to see the entire place. They weren't finished building the last time I was here."

"My daughter and her friend were more thrilled about my trip than I was after looking at the resort's website," she admitted, quelling the urge to kick off her shoes and dash into the frothy waves.

She'd never been a spontaneous kind of person and became even more reticent after John's death. The impulse to do something for the sheer physical pleasure of the act and the soulful joy of being fully in the moment pleased and frightened her.

She was here to receive an award. No matter how decadent the resort was, she must not let her inner childlike curiosity out to play. Maybe she'd find a few private moments to explore and indulge, but now wasn't the time. She curled her hands into fists, then slowly relaxed them, refocusing herself. "My daughter mentioned there are four siblings, each handling a different aspect of operations. I can't wait to meet them."

"All of them are good people. Zoey and her sister Sam were terrific to work with." Wade stared into her eyes. "Like you."

Sherry involuntarily rolled her bottom lip between her teeth. "What a nice thing to say."

"It's true. And I'm glad you like the resort." He held her gaze a bit longer, but she didn't mind. She liked seeing his sadness disappear.

"Peace, magic, relaxation." Sherry went with her gut. "It's like I can smell it in the air. The cedar and pine trees. The rich, earthy scent of soil. The tangy brine of the ocean." She closed her eyes. "I might be imagining it, but I smell eucalyptus and the sweetness of flowers. Maybe the grapes from the vineyard."

He chuckled, and she flushed, embarrassed by her exaggerated reaction.

"I'm sorry," he said. "I didn't mean to embarrass you. It's so...refreshing...to see such an enthusiastic and uninhibited expression of pleasure when you're usually so self-contained."

Would he laugh at her?

Think her passion foolish?

She hoped not and gulped down her anxiety and gathered her courage. "Aromas are my hobby." She chuckled at the confusion on his face and explained. "I'm forever mixing and experimenting with new scent profiles. I make organic beauty and bath products in my spare time. It was a hobby years ago, and I picked it up again after my husband died. Since I again started following my desire to make the perfect skin care products, I find myself sniffing the air like a hound dog and studying how aromas affect people."

Wade's eyes shifted to focus on a point over her shoulder. She turned to see Kimberly, his executive assistant, the one she'd gotten to know during the last system implementation, waving in their direction from the main building.

"You're a fascinating woman, Sherry Kline." His voice carried a husky note of admiration, but his gaze remained pinned on Kimberly. "I'm being summoned. Looks like I'm back on duty. Will I see you at the reception tonight?"

Did she detect a note of hopefulness in his question?

"Of course." Sizzling awareness made it hard to keep her tone casual.

She scribbled a mental note with the words *He's Your Boss!* written in bold and double underlined. Wade was a very attractive, very kind, very sexy man who was also very much hands off.

"Great. I look forward to seeing you then." He nodded before striding toward Kimberly.

Sherry watched until they disappeared into the resort, doing her best to ignore the gaping sense of emptiness left in the wake of Wade's departure.

"You can register at the front desk right through there." Alex pointed in the same direction Wade had gone. "I'll see that your luggage is delivered so you can settle in. Enjoy your stay at the Silver Fox Resort, Mrs. Kline."

For the first time since learning of the award and her week-long vacation, anticipation washed over Sherry, leaving her enthused and invigorated.

A large bronze sculpture of a leaping stag caught her eye as she admired the landscaping around the building. The architecture and grounds combined to create the impression of understated elegance. Passing through the same massive dark wood doors Wade had entered, she discovered a well-appointed lobby. As she approached the front counter, an attractive young woman dressed in a neat uniform greeted her. The receptionist's name tag read *Amy Denham*.

"Welcome to Silver Fox Resort. You must be Sherry Kline. Mr. Briggs said you were on your way in. I hope you had an uneventful flight and a relaxing ride." Amy's friendly manner immediately set Sherry at ease.

"It's my first trip to California," she admitted. "It was nice to see some of the area, and Alex provided outstanding customer service. He's very personable."

As Amy processed her registration, Sherry took in the wood beams bracing the ceiling, the massive stone fireplace, and the handcrafted redwood coffee tables. She wanted to do a little celebratory shimmy to acknowledge her small but important achievements—making the trip, conversing with Wade, and opening herself up to the possibility of.... She wasn't entirely sure what she was opening herself up to, but after three years of a white-knuckled grip on life, trying to regain a sense of control, she was ready to loosen her hold. Ready to sit back and let life happen instead of forcing events into a specific sequence.

Now more than ever, she was determined to enjoy her stay at the resort. And she'd get through it without crashing into a table or showing up at an event late or saying something silly.

"You're all set," Amy said, handing her a keycard in a small holder imprinted with the resort's logo. "We'll deliver your luggage shortly. If you need anything, just let us know. Martin, please show Mrs. Kline to her cottage."

A neatly uniformed young man who reminded her of Tyler grinned and motioned for her to follow him.

"Thank you for your help, Amy." Sherry hiked her purse onto her shoulder and turned to follow the bellman.

Martin led the way from the main building to a path that wrapped around the complex. With each twist and turn, she was thankful for a guide. After a few minutes, Martin stopped in front of a rustic cottage.

"Behind you is the main center of the complex. To the right is the spa and pool, and farther down you'll find a walkway leading to the meeting rooms and business center. The reception is being held there. Here's a map." She accepted the brightly colored trifold he handed her. "If you visit the meditation gardens, we ask that you keep talking to a minimum. The lap pool is down by the gardens, as is the art center. Your personalized itinerary is in your room. Do you have questions or need anything at the moment?"

Her head spun. The profusion of flowers fronting her cottage scented the air. Vibrant butterflies hovered above the greenery. In every direction she looked, there was an area begging to be explored.

This really is a magical place.

"I'm good for now. Thank you," she said.

"Okay." He nodded as if confirming a mission accomplished. "If you do have questions, dial five, and one of the staff will be happy to assist you."

Martin retreated down the pathway, leaving her to admire the setting. Climbing the stairs to a tiny porch, Sherry slipped the keycard into the locking mechanism. The door opened to reveal a spacious room painted in warm shades of cream and pale green. Plush area rugs covered the marble tile floor, and leather furniture marked a seating area. She admired the artwork and brass lighting fixtures, each detail adding up to create an inviting haven. She peeked into the spacious bathroom, promising herself a leisurely soak in the huge tub, then proceeded to the bedroom. A mound of pillows adorned the king-size bed draped in flowy fabric. She toed off her flats, threw out her arms, and fell backwards onto the bed, laughing.

What was I afraid of? This is heaven.

She rolled her head toward the large sliding glass door that looked out toward the ocean, wondering where Wade was at that moment and replaying their conversation in her head. Too excited to remain still, she scrambled off the bed and went to explore the rest of the cottage.

A large fruit basket on the kitchenette counter drew her attention. She slipped the card out of its envelope, her belly fluttering when her eyes fell upon Wade's name at the bottom of the card. Her pulse quickened as the image of Wade's handsome face flashed across her mind. Delight filled her heart.

What a nice man.

She dropped the card on the counter, trying to downplay her reaction. *There's no need to read too much into this.* It wasn't like Wade personally presented her with the gift basket. *Kimberly probably sent fruit baskets to all the North American division winners on Wade's behalf.*

She sighed. How was she ever going to be able to navigate dating again when she melted the first time an attractive man was nice to her?

A knock sounded on her door, interrupting her thoughts.

"A minute, please," Sherry called as she strolled to the door, opened it, and stepped aside for Martin to wheel in her bags. "Thank you."

"You're welcome, ma'am." She reached toward her purse, but he shook his head. "No, ma'am. The resort is gratuity-free. Enjoy your stay."

As she was about to close the door, the sound of Wade's voice drifted to her ears.

"When did this happen?"

"Mr. Flannigan sent me an email this morning." Sherry recognized Kimberly's voice even though her high-pitched words held a sharp degree of panic. "He's rearranged the entire schedule. How am I supposed to manage this when I'm already dealing with several other problems?"

Sherry peeked out the front door. Wade and Kimberly walked slowly down the path, their heads angled over a single piece of paper. Worry lines marred his forehead, and Kimberly looked distraught, her hair in disarray and her face chalk white.

"Have you spoken to Nate Keller, the chef, about changing the menu for the award ceremony?" Wade asked, his voice tense.

"He's busy right now, but Zoey Foster told me he'll be available after the cocktail reception this evening."

Sherry had hosted dinner parties for John's clients all the time, but she hadn't thrown a party since he passed away. Those small gatherings took days of planning. She couldn't imagine how much organization went into a week-long event like this corporate trip. She empathized with the concern splashed across Kimberly's face.

"I hope there won't be any problem because time isn't on our side. Mr. Flannigan will arrive soon, and I want everything to be flawless. Nothing can go wrong. We *have* to make a positive impression." Wade's voice dropped. "You know what's riding on this. I can't give the man any excuse to say no."

"Yes, sir." Kimberly's shoulders pressed back with determination then dropped in defeat.

The wild, stricken look in the younger woman's eyes worried Sherry. An alarm bell rang in her head. Sherry understood the burden of being deluged with problems and having the weight of too much responsibility resting on your shoulders.

"Everything must be perfect, Kimberly." Wade repeated the statement as if life and death hung in the balance of how well the award retreat went off. "If there is anything I need to know, tell me immediately."

"Sir...there's...there's another problem," Kimberly stuttered.

"Spit it out. It can't be that bad." Wade folded his arms across his chest.

"Well..." Kimberly hesitated. "Some of the employees missed their flights. We're trying to make alternative arrangements now. And Mrs. Flannigan changed her mind about attending. Again. As of last week, she wasn't coming. In his email, Mr. Flannigan said she's decided to join him, which means all of the seating charts need to be changed and I need to assemble her itinerary."

"First things first. Let's make sure the award recipients get here, then work on the seating charts. Tonight's reception is buffet-style, so no issue there. The dinner isn't until tomorrow. Talk to whoever is coordinating logistics for the resort and enlist their help. Squeezing in one more chair shouldn't be a big deal." Wade rubbed his hand over the back of his neck and rolled his shoulders. "Anything else?"

Kimberly cringed. "One of the crystal awards shattered in transit."

"Call the office and have a replacement shipped overnight." He patted Kimberly's shoulder. "Last-minute problems are inherent so stay calm and deal with things one at a time."

"This event has lots of moving parts, and I'm a little overwhelmed," she admitted.

Sherry's heart ached watching Wade and Kimberly

struggle. Managing projects wasn't as easy as it seemed. She always had a Plan B, C, and D. Right now, Wade needed a plan to salvage the situation, and Kimberly was clearly in over her head.

"You're doing fine, Kimberly. It's just that we can't afford to make mistakes. Our employees' livelihoods are on the line."

Sherry's breath hitched in her throat.

Had Wade just confirmed her worst fears?

The thought of losing not only her income but the stability and routine she'd meticulously cultivated made her nauseous.

Our employees' livelihoods are on the line.

What did that mean?

Were entire units being sold off? Divisions being closed?

Was the company downsizing? Putting a freeze on raises and new hires?

The implications were horrible, not just for herself but every employee.

She didn't understand what this event had to do with preserving jobs, but she wasn't the type to stand by when help was needed. Without a second thought, she was out of the cottage, chasing Wade and Kimberly down the pathway.

"Excuse me." Her footsteps faltered as she got closer, and she started second-guessing her decision to butt in. Too late now, she thought. "I couldn't help but overhear your conversation when you passed by my cottage. Is there something I can help with? Maybe the travel changes that need to be made or reorganizing the seating charts?"

Wade and Kimberly stared at her like she'd suddenly grown horns out of her head.

"Thank you, but I don't need any help." Kimberly clutched a binder to her chest like a shield.

Oh, but the young woman did need help. She was too

insecure to realize Sherry didn't want to make her look bad. She just wanted to resolve whatever threatened her fellow coworkers' jobs.

"Sherry"—Wade stepped around Kimberly—"your kind gesture is appreciated, but you're not here to work. My assistant has everything under control, don't you?"

The frazzled young woman's face crumpled than smoothed out with a too-bright expression of agreement. Sherry realized she was right about Kimberly needing assistance.

"You can never have too much help with a big event like this," Sherry pressed. "It'll be no trouble at all. Let me know what you'd like me to do, and I'll help." She was careful to phrase her offer so it didn't come across like she was trying to take over.

"I—" Kimberly started.

Sherry kept her eyes on Wade, silently hoping he wouldn't turn down her offer. When he shook his head, her heart dropped.

"Sherry, this vacation is a reward for your hard work this past year. You're supposed to take a break. None of the other employees will be working."

"Frankly, that's what I'm worried about." Her gaze jumped from Wade to Kimberly. "There's no way I can relax, knowing Kimberly is juggling all these last-minutes complications. If I handle the seating charts, she can take care of the travelers and attend to Mr. and Mrs. Flannigan. Once Kimberly has everything under control, we can all relax."

Relief and gratitude shone on Kimberly's face. Her shoulders relaxed, and she loosened the death grip on the planning binder.

"Sherry, I don't think—" Wade said.

Sherry held up a hand to stop Wade from having to come

up with an excuse. It was time to tell the truth, or this ping-pong conversation would continue and she wasn't about to lose the match. "I overheard your conversation about jobs being on the line. I'm sorry. I didn't mean to eavesdrop, but my luggage was just being dropped off and I couldn't help but hear what was said. I'd really like to help."

"I could use another set of hands," Kimberly finally admitted.

Wade lowered his head, his gaze sliding away from hers.

Panic threatened to choke her airway, but she swallowed against the fear.

"Thank you, Sherry." Wade finally met her eyes, his brows furrowed in dismay. "I'll find a way to make this up to you."

Saving my job would be a good start.

Chapter 6

*W*ade brushed his apprehension aside and sauntered into the cocktail reception with a confident stride. A few feet into the room, he paused to scope out the scene.

Strands of white fairy lights created a festive ambiance. High-top tables adorned with crisp white linen were strategically placed throughout the room, inviting people to cluster in small groups. Colorful bouquets of fresh flowers added a touch of elegance and softened the rustic architecture of dark wooden timbers, tall windows, and creamy stucco walls.

He spotted Sherry talking to one of his direct reports, laughing at something Dave said. Wade could see she was charming the man, and he was proud she seemed to have tucked away her shyness.

After Sherry handled the seating arrangements, she was able to help Kimberly problem-solve the travel delays, and worked smoothly with the airlines, the resort staff, and the frustrated travelers. Her willingness to pitch in filled him with awe. He rarely came across a woman as kind or as selfless as Sherry. In a way, she reminded him of who he tried to be.

She'd exchanged her skirt and sweater for a knee-length, bold red wrap dress which showed off her legs. The fabric hugged her figure and provided a contrast to her dark blond hair. There was nothing blatantly provocative about the dress, but Wade admired the classy way it accented her curves.

She was stunning.

Pulse racing, he adjusted his tie and continued watching her graceful movements until his conscience gave him a swift kick.

What was he thinking?

Sherry Kline was off-limits.

She was an employee.

Although, that argument would no longer hold water if Flannigan sold off the Des Moines unit. While she was with the company, they'd remain coworkers. Boss and subordinate. At best, casual friends. Nothing more.

He strode toward her. She must have sensed him coming because she turned and their eyes met. She smiled without hesitation. His heart slammed against his ribs, hard, as a thrill went through him. Golden curls fell loosely, framing her face and tumbling over her shoulders. With the tousled hair and curve-hugging dress, she looked like a woman ready for a night out on the town, not the brisk, efficient project manager he worked with.

"Hi, Sherry." He couldn't help the husky drop to his voice.

"Hello." She flicked an approving glance over him and then leaned to the side and glanced toward the room's entrance. "Stuart Flannigan just arrived."

He turned to watch the corporate CEO strut into the room with an elegantly dressed brunette on his arm. Flannigan was a tall man with wide shoulders and a stocky build. In his late fifties, his sandy brown hair was going silver at the temples and his sharp gray eyes were hooded by saggy eyelids.

The newest Mrs. Flannigan—new because she was wife number five—wore a sleeveless black sequined dress that showed off a figure enhanced by plastic surgery. She looked to be in her late twenties or early thirties and was thin to the point of emaciation, with pronounced cheekbones and hollow cheeks. The only roundness on her frame were artificially proportioned hips, butt, and boobs. Despite the heavy makeup, it was easy to see she was at least twenty years younger than her husband, who also happened to be the son of the chairman of the board for Stallion Protection Partners.

Wade threw a warning look at Sherry as he waited for the man of the hour to approach. She blinked twice, calm and steady, silently assuring him he could trust her. Together, they watched Flannigan and his wife work the room, accepting greetings and exchanging introductions. As they drew closer, Wade panicked. He could not recall Mrs. Flannigan's first name, and his boss was the type of guy to make an insult out of even the smallest lapse.

Crap, what was the woman's name?

Ellen? No, that was one or two wives back. Carrie? Colleen? Something with a C.

"Briggs! There you are!" Flannigan called in a loud voice, chest puffed out.

"Good evening, Stuart. I'm so glad your lovely wife—"

"Caroline," Sherry whispered.

"—Caroline was able to join you at the last minute." The two men exchanged a brief handshake. Wade turned slightly. "Caroline, this is Sherry Kline. She's the Employee of the Year winner from our Des Moines office."

"It's a pleasure to meet you, Mr. and Mrs. Flannigan."

Sherry moved into the inner circle. "What a beautiful dress. I'm afraid your husband is going to have trouble keeping everyone's attention with such a stunning woman at his side."

Caroline's haughty look softened, and she bent to confide something to Sherry which Wade couldn't hear. Shaking her head, Sherry responded in a conspiratorial tone. "What do men know? Of course, the dress and jewelry aren't too over the top. We're in California where men wear sneakers with their tuxedos. Surely, a woman can wear a floor-length beaded gown for a corporate cocktail party."

Caroline's coy smile turned into an authentic grin.

"How was your flight, Mr. Flannigan?" Sherry maintained an air of ease. "Travel can be exhausting."

"We flew here on my new private jet. All the comforts of home, including a king-size bed and shower." Stuart's accented tone was blatantly arrogant. "I named her after my lovely wife." He patted Caroline's arm. "She deserves only the best."

"Oh, darling." Caroline fluttered three-inch fake eyelashes. "You always make me feel so special." She turned to Sherry. "Stuart named his new yacht *Caroline* as well. If you've ever flown on a private jet, I'm sure you'll agree the experience is divine. I'll never fly commercial again."

"I don't mind commercial flights." Sherry traded looks with Wade. "It's an opportunity to meet new people." The way she crafted her statement made him certain she was thinking about their shuttle ride from the airport to the resort, *their* opportunity to get better acquainted. "You're more fortune than most people, Mrs. Flannigan, to have a choice about how you travel. I imagine you're very grateful to be so blessed."

Wade almost did a double take. Had Sherry just snubbed the head honcho's wife or was her comment innocent? From the confused look on Caroline's face, she wasn't certain what to make of Sherry's comment either.

"Stuart works very hard for his success and wealth," the woman finally said.

"Most people do," Sherry said softly. "It's rewarding to have one's efforts recognized. I appreciate how the company validated my contributions and value by including me in this event."

Her simple statement strengthened Wade's determination to convince the CEO not to sell out. His plan had merit and good odds for success. The downside was that it required time for poorly performing units to recoup their losses through alternative strategies. Stuart was not known for his patience or altruism. The only way he would approve Wade's plan was if there was something that directly benefited Stuart.

The CEO and his wife glided off toward the bar as Wade and Sherry exchanged a private look that made him want to whisk her off into the moonlight. Today, he'd started to see Sherry Kline, the extraordinary woman. She confronted her fears, large and small, overcame tragedy to hold her family together, and pitched in when others needed help. She was so much more than most women he knew.

Wade hadn't intentionally avoided dating after his divorce, but he hadn't met anyone who seemed compatible. Now, at the very worst time, the least suitable woman was triggering fantasies about slow dancing on the beach, sharing carryout Chinese at the end of a long workweek, and spooning together between cozy flannel sheets on a snowy Denver night.

The moment was broken when a trio of women eased into the space vacated by the Flannigans. They introduced themselves and began exchanging stories about their jobs with the company, family, hobbies, and effusive praise for the accommodations.

"Have you tried the bath products provided by the resort?" Sherry asked, her tone deepening with enthusiasm Wade didn't understand until he remembered her interest in making organic soaps and potions. "They're handcrafted by local artisans, using all natural ingredients."

"Who has time for that?" One woman dismissed the idea with a wave of her hand. "I'm sure it's not as good as the skin care regimen I purchase at the department store. Six hundred dollars for a three-month supply of cleanser, toner, eye serum, and moisturizing lotion guaranteed to reverse the effects of aging."

"I want to know what you're using," a slender Asian woman Wade recognized from the Miami office commented to Sherry. "Your skin is lovely, and if I'm not mistaken, you aren't wearing a bit of foundation or blush."

"Oh, the products I use are very exclusive." Sherry's expression was serious, but Wade recognized the sassy spark in her eyes. "They're only available in Des Moines and not for sale to the public."

After teasing the women for a few minutes, she finally revealed that she'd concocted an organic anti-aging formula she made at home using olive oil, shea butter, and six different essential oils.

Chuckling to himself, Wade wandered off to the bar for a drink and waited until the cluster of women around Sherry finally dispersed before rejoining her.

Her smile turned to a grimace, and she went up on tiptoe, revealing well-shaped calves.

"Are you alright?" Wade asked.

"These shoes are killing me," Sherry replied, giving him an apologetic look. "I need to get off my feet. However, I don't want to leave yet because my disappearing might seem rude. I haven't even been here an hour."

"Don't worry about it," Wade said. "This is a mixer. Some of the people aren't even here yet, thanks to the travel delays. You aren't punching a time clock this week. I say we blow this popsicle stand."

Sherry giggled, and Wade felt much younger than his forty-five years. With a backwards glance at Flannigan, Wade offered Sherry his elbow.

She hooked her hand through it. "Where are we off to?"

"To the bar for a nightcap. Kick your shoes off under the table. I won't tell anyone," Wade said gallantly. "After you, please."

"Thank you for understanding." Her smile heated his blood.

They walked from the meeting facilities to the main resort building. A few couples were seated around the polished bar, but most of the tables were unoccupied. He allowed Sherry to select a secluded four-top, pulling out her chair and making sure she was comfortably seated. He slid into the chair across from her as a brawny bartender with black hair clipped short approached to take their order.

"Good evening, folks. What can I get you?"

Wade looked to Sherry, waiting for her to order first.

"Chardonnay, please." She tucked a small evening bag onto her lap.

"Scotch on the rocks for me," Wade said, providing his room information so the bartender could charge the order to his account.

A few minutes later, the bartender returned with their drinks as well as two glasses of ice water. Wade swirled the amber liquid in his glass, content to watch Sherry sip her wine.

"This peace and quiet is a nice change after all the chatter and laughter at the party." Wade sighed with pleasure. He liked people. Liked being with them and celebrating with them, but stress and the last-minute time crush to prepare for the trip had worn him out.

"I agree." Sherry's light feminine laugh made him glad they were alone. "The cocktail reception was great, but I'm not accustomed to being 'on' for such large social events."

"I'm happy I won't have to engage in another conversation about yachts and planes," he added.

Sherry giggled, the tip of her tongue darting out to capture a drop of wine on her lower lip.

"You were amazing back there." He held her gaze.

She blushed, twirling the stem of her wineglass between her fingers. "It's nice to know all those years being a corporate wife and hostess aren't going to waste."

They stared at each other, a little longer this time, prompting Wade to give in to curiosity. "What motivates you to work so hard, Sherry?"

She considered his question before responding. "Honestly? I was raised with a strong work ethic. But after John died…everything was about control. I worked hard to control what was happening to me. Control outcomes. Not be subject to sudden, unpredictable change. I wanted to create stability and predictability for Alison and Tyler, but now I realize I needed it as much as they did. This job probably saved my life." She examined the golden liquid before taking a small gulp. "It definitely saved my sanity."

"You're a remarkable woman. I've never met anyone like you. You're so open and honest."

Sherry leaned in a little, her fragrance filling his nostrils. When their eyes met again, his pulse quickened.

"By the way, you look great." He raised his brows. "I hope that doesn't cross any lines."

"I noticed earlier how nice you look," she admitted,

humor creasing the corners of her eyes. "Am I crossing any lines?"

The tension between them flared, electricity sparking inside him. Wade cleared his throat, and the spell of the moment was broken.

"Do you ever take a break?" Sherry's forehead creased into a slight frown. "You have an assistant, but you seem to work harder than everyone else."

Wade shrugged. "That strong work ethic is something we have in common. I believe in leading by example. I don't expect my employees to work as many hours as I do, but the most profitable companies are those whose employees are personally invested in a successful outcome." Creating an environment where his staff could achieve personal success was the cornerstone of his management philosophy.

If Flannigan refused to approve Wade's employee-retention plan and sold off units, including the Des Moines office, Wade didn't know how he'd be able to stay on. How could he lead a company that valued money over people?

"Stallion has had some challenges on that front," she said carefully. "Our unit has carried a negative balance the last two years, but it isn't because the people there aren't hardworking, dedicated employees. We've all done our best to reduce expenses and increase revenue."

"I'm aware of that."

Wade lifted his glass but then set it back down, thinking of his kids, his career, his life, all parading by him in a flicker of a moment.

"I've been considering my future." He inhaled deeply, releasing all the air from his lungs before continuing. "I'm not getting any younger, and my boys are growing up fast. I'd like to spend more time with them. I haven't told anyone else yet, Sherry, but I've been considering stepping down, possibly retiring or finding a consulting position."

"What? Why?" Sherry's face paled. "You're too young to retire. And you seem too responsible to up and leave Stallion. So many people depend on you."

"True. I wouldn't just leave." He did his best to defuse her surprise. "But I don't want to get to the end of my life and have regrets, and Stuart may not give me a choice." He let the comment dangle between them.

Chapter 7

While the rest of the Stallion guests and executives enjoyed the Silver Fox Resort amenities, Sherry, Kimberly, and Wade tag-teamed final preparations for the award reception to be held that evening.

With help from Zoey Foster, the resort owner, and her staff, every detail was checked and double checked so the banquet would be impeccable.

Sherry suggested the idea to project the company logo onto the back wall of the room, an effort she was sure Stuart Flannigan would be impressed by. After a brief conversation with Wade and learning more about his mission to preserve jobs, she agreed appealing to Flannigan's corporate pride was a smart strategy.

"I'd like to go over the menu one more time before I head back to the kitchen." Zoey tapped a pen against the pad in her hand as she scanned the tablecloths, place settings, and flower arrangements.

"Before guests are seated, servers will circulate through the room with trays of mushroom crostini, lamb lollipops, and bacon-wrapped scallops." Sherry glanced at her printout.

"Dessert options include white and dark chocolate cheesecake," Kimberly chimed in, skimming the notes in her binder. "Lavender-infused lemon sorbet, and fresh fruit cups drizzled with honey from the Silver Fox Resort beehives."

"We've agreed to leave the appetizers to Nate, right?" Zoey asked.

"Yes." Sherry nodded. "I was blown away by the canapés I had at last night's reception. You have a very talented husband."

"The way to a woman's heart and all that." Zoey beamed. "Will you be making any changes to the cocktail menu?"

"No, the wine and mixers are perfect."

Kimberly's phone chimed and she frowned. "Excuse me. I need to take this."

"Sure, go ahead." Sherry turned back to Zoey. "I see you were able to add another table without too much trouble."

"Yes." Zoey looked toward the back of the room. "The tables are closer than preferrable but still within the fire code."

A muffled cry pulled Sherry's attention to Kimberly, who had tears streaking down her face.

"Oh no, what's wrong?" Sherry asked, rushing to the young woman's side and guiding her into a chair.

"It's Grammy. She slipped in the bathroom and fell. The neighbor called an ambulance. They think she broke her hip." Kimberly's entire body trembled. "Grammy raised me after my mom died. She's the only family I have."

Zoey hurried over with a glass of water. "Drink this. Take a few deep breaths. We'll help you get this figured out."

"I should go home, but I can't leave." Kimberly's wild eyes skidded around the room.

"No, you have to go," Sherry assured her. "Your grandmother needs you."

"But I'm needed here, too," Kimberly's voice rose to a high shrill piercing complaint.

"Everything's been finalized. Amy, Zoey, and I can handle things from here." Sherry's voice broke off as Wade came into the room.

His eyes jumped to Sherry and then over to Kimberly. "What happened?"

His lightning-fast appraisal of the situation and calm response impressed Sherry. This was the kind of man you wanted around when things got rough.

"My grandmother fell." Kimberly drew in a hitching breath and mimicked her boss's composed demeanor as best she could. "She's in surgery now."

"We need to get you home." Wade's expression softened sympathetically. "Go pack. I'll see about a flight."

"We can't afford any problems. Remember?" Kimberly reminded him.

"What's left to be done?" Wade unbuttoned his cuffs and began rolling up the sleeves of his blue Oxford shirt, revealing muscular forearms.

Calm and *capable. How was this man still single?*

"Thanks to Sherry and Zoey and Amy, everything is in place," Kimberly confessed. "It's just making sure the event goes as planned and handling any last-minute complications. After tonight, there's very little the hotel staff can't handle."

"That's true," Amy added, joining the huddle. "We've got all hands on deck to ensure everything goes smoothly for the award ceremony and the rest of the week's activities. I guarantee your guests will have a top-notch experience here."

"Kimberly, I admire your dedication to the job," Wade said, "but your grandmother comes first. Family should always be your number one priority. Besides, if you remain here, your mind will be on the problems at home. You won't be of any use to anyone."

"You're probably right." Kimberly seemed calmer now that a solution had been found.

Sherry's heart melted a little at Wade's insistence that Kimberly leave to be with her grandmother. Not all bosses were as accommodating or as compassionate as Wade. She understood why employees respected him and how he inspired so much loyalty. Too bad he wasn't Global CEO of Stallion Protection Partners. His integrity and regard for the company's workforce revealed a man who cared deeply about others.

She hoped some of that would rub off on Stuart Flannigan when he finalized his decision about the future of the corporation.

"Will you need a ride from the airport when you get back to Denver?" Amy asked. "I can arrange a car for you when I call our travel agency to book the flight."

"Oh, yes. I hadn't even thought about that." Kimberly stood and wiped away her tears. "If they can take me straight to the hospital, I'd appreciate it. I won't stop worrying until I see Grammy for myself."

Amy laid her arm around the young woman's shoulders and escorted her from the dining room.

Zoey gave Sherry an apologetic look when her phone rang. "I'm late for a meeting. Text if you need anything or tell Amy. She has my schedule for the rest of the afternoon."

"Sherry can bring me up to speed." Wade waved as Zoey scurried through the maze of tables.

"What do you think?" Sherry asked, gesturing at the décor.

"I'm impressed. Again, I'm sorry you're working on what's supposed to be—"

Approaching footsteps interrupted their evaluation of the setup as Stuart Flannigan entered the spacious room.

"Briggs, there you are!" he bellowed.

"Is something wrong?" Wade asked.

"I just ran into one of the assistants. I think it's your girl. She's supposed to be the point of contact for this event, but she just told me she's leaving. Who gave her permission to bail on one of the most prestigious events of the year?" Stuart frowned. "She created a scene in front of several other resort guests. That's not how Stallion employees conduct themselves. Process her termination as soon as you're back in your office."

"Her termination? Stuart, Kimberly just received word of a family emergency." Wade's low, controlled words were a dramatic contrast to Flannigan's loud complaints. "I not only granted permission for her to leave, I insisted on it."

"Unless someone is on their deathbed, she should have stuck around. She's showing no dedication to this company, and I demand loyalty." Stuart wagged a finger, his face scrunched in an expression of anger.

Wade, whose jaw was clenched, narrowed his eyes.

"Her grandmother fell and is undergoing emergency surgery," Wade repeated. "Her departure will not impact the event in any way, I can assure you."

Sherry's pulse raced as she observed Wade's self-control in the face of extreme foolishness.

"Keep your employees in check, Briggs," Stuart grumbled. "I came to inform you that I can't sit through a bunch of boring thank-you speeches from every single winner. I've been on the go since ten o'clock this morning and jet lag is catching up with me."

Every muscle in Wade's face tightened and his chest expanded as he drew in a slow, controlled breath before speaking. "The award recipients were invited to prepare a brief acknowledgement. We asked them to indicate if they planned to speak and there are less than eleven people who accepted the invitation. I'm sure it won't take more than thirty or forty minutes for that part of the program."

"No one ever sticks to the schedule." Flannigan's lower lip jutted out like a spoiled child. "You're asking me to endure an hour of hot air as they repeat the same thing over and over. 'Thank you to my wife.' 'Thank you to my husband.' 'Thank you to my dog, Bingo.' They never should have been offered the opportunity. Whose brilliant idea was that anyhow?"

"That was part of the event overview issued by Stallion's chairman of the board." Wade barely contained his smirk.

"M-my father mandated speeches for the winners?" Flannigan sputtered and then his eyes narrowed. "Cancel it anyway. My father isn't here. He'll never know."

"Mr. Briggs." Sherry interrupted the conversation politely with a deferential tone she didn't usually use. "The audiovisual technician confirmed the equipment is set up for the live broadcast of tonight's award ceremony. I sent the access information to headquarters, and Mrs. Seton in Human Resources said an email would be sent out to every Stallion employee so they can watch the event."

Stuart Flannigan pivoted slowly on his heel to face Sherry, dragging his eyes up and down in a disapproving manner. "Another dictate from my father?"

"I'm not sure, sir." Sherry's dislike for the man doubled. "I do know my colleagues at the Des Moines unit are very excited about the real-time broadcast."

"Fine," Flannigan snapped. "But you'd better have someone tracking time and keeping the program on schedule."

"Will do. Was that all, sir?" Wade's anger was obvious in the way he bit off each word.

As far as Sherry knew, he still hadn't spoken to Flannigan

about his proposal to save jobs. Flannigan had lost this round, and an egocentric personality like that didn't do well when his pride took a blow. She had to do something to help the man save face or Wade didn't stand a chance. Flannigan would nix his idea before Wade even got the words out of his mouth.

"You'll be seated on the dais where the recipients cross to receive their awards and speak a few words." She forced an admiring smile. "This is an excellent opportunity for employees to see company leadership in action. What a privilege to receive an award from the CEO himself of one of the most widely recognized international insurance companies. Everyone will be talking about you, sir. Many know you by name, but not by face."

"Hmm." Flannigan's spine straightened and the flush across his cheeks began to fade "How many employees are expected to tune in?"

Probably less than a dozen, Sherry thought, but Flannigan didn't need to know that.

"Last year's annual report stated Stallion employs more than ten thousand people around the world." Sherry widened her eyes. "So, potentially, you could be connecting with ten thousand employees."

"Fine." Flannigan's shirt, stretched tight across his puffed-up chest, no longer gapped between the buttonholes as his chest deflated a few degrees. "There is the matter of the seating arrangements. My wife is displeased with the order and wants it reconfigured." He thrust a sheet of paper toward Sherry. "Handle this, please."

"Of course, Mr. Flannigan." Sherry looked at the scribble of arrows and rectangles. "It's a shame our employees won't have a chance to see what a beautiful woman your new wife is. In fact, with these changes, you'll no longer be onscreen either."

"What?" He grabbed the paper back, scanned it, and ripped it in half. "The seating arrangement stands. Caroline is new to life as a corporate spouse. It's time she learned sometimes sacrifices have to be made for the sake of the company."

"Too bad all of our employees aren't as talented and skilled as Mrs.—" Flannigan paused, clearly having no clue who he was talking to.

"Mrs. Kline," Wade provided. "She is exceptional, but the majority of our employees are outstanding."

"Well done, Mrs. Kline." Flannigan nodded, as if he'd proposed the live broadcast, employee speeches, and the seating arrangement. "I trust I can pass along one last request and leave it in your capable hands?"

"Of course," she said, gritting her teeth as she smiled.

"My daughter and a few friends arrived this morning from LA. She'd like a band at tonight's event. We'll turn it into a dinner dance. Won't that be fun?" Flannigan guffawed and then pivoted toward the door. He glanced over his shoulder. "Briggs, you look like hell. Take some time off when you get back."

"Did he just say his daughter wants a band?" Wade's tone was dangerously quiet. "He's turning this into the Stuart Flannigan Show instead of a well-deserved reward for our top-performing employees. That includes you."

"Don't worry about me." Warmth spread throughout her body at Wade's concern. "Stuart Flannigan is a self-centered windbag. I've handled plenty of corporate blowhards like him. It's all about stroking his ego and making him feel like the BMOC."

"Big man on campus?" Wade's rigid posture relaxed. "I haven't heard that phrase in ages."

"I'm showing my age." Sherry dropped her eyes shyly, feeling like a young woman at her first dance instead of a worldly widowed woman. Wade had a way of making her feel young and beautiful, with a bright future ahead of her.

"I like your age." His eyes darkened with appreciation. "You're solid, grounded. Confident in who you are and what you value. Comfortable in your own skin without the need for pretentious trappings."

"Like plastic surgery and boats named after me?" She couldn't resist the dig.

"Exactly." His expression shifted, becoming serious. "Thank you, Sherry, for coming to my rescue. I was so angry over Flannigan's ridiculous demands I almost ruined my chance to present my proposal to him. If you hadn't stepped in, I suspect Flannigan would have given *me* the axe. I'm tempted to resign this very minute and put all of this stress behind me, as it is."

"Don't do it, Wade." Sherry clutched his forearm with both hands. "If you want to leave the company, I respect that. But if you walk out now, you'll never forgive yourself."

"You're right." Wade covered her hands with his. "What would I do without you, Sherry? I mean, what would the company do without you? I'd still like to find a way to repay you for your kindness."

"Repay me by not resigning and saving our jobs." She forced herself to loosen her grip but kept hold of Wade, loving the strong, warm feel of him.

He nodded and worked up a smile, but she spotted the sadness in his eyes before he looked away.

Chapter 8

*W*ade paced the length of his villa, panic cutting through him with each step he took. He adjusted his bow tie and then readjusted it as if he hadn't gotten it right the first time. He stepped in front of the wall-length mirror in the bathroom to check his appearance again.

He stepped out of the bathroom, grabbed his jacket, and headed for the door. The walk down the path to the banquet room provided a chance to steady his nerves and regain his composure. He hoped, for everyone's sake, Flannigan would save his dramatics for another place and time. The employees deserved this moment, and the man's need for attention should not overshadow their accomplishments.

His eyes widened as he stepped into the banquet hall. By day, it looked elegant and impressive. Under the golden light of the chandeliers overhead, it had been transformed into a regal, magical setting. The table linens glowed. The hydrangea and delphinium centerpieces scented the air with a light floral aroma. Instrumental dinner music was barely audible beneath the murmur of conversation and tinkle of glassware.

He inspected the room, registering the display of awards, including a replacement for the one broken in transit, the video camera in the back of the room for the live broadcast, and Mike McMann standing with his wife, the last of the delayed travelers. It appeared all crises had been averted.

He had one more crisis to deal with, but that would have to wait until he was able to meet privately with Flannigan.

His thoughts about the potential lost jobs and selfish CEO got displaced when he caught sight of Sherry. She stood, poised and relaxed, laughing and chatting with other guests, a glass of white wine in one hand. She was a stunning vision in a silk navy blue pantsuit, her hair rippling in curls around her shoulders. He liked this softer, more feminine look better than her tidy professional appearance. His body temperature soared, despite the cool air circulating through the room.

Resisting the urge to join the cluster of people around her, Wade circulated through the room, congratulating winners and being introduced to spouses. As much as he wished he and Sherry were staying at the Silver Fox Resort together, he was here as an executive officer of Stallion Protection Partners for a corporate event. He had a legitimate excuse to speak with Sherry, but he'd claim that privilege later. After the corporate Employee of the Year winner was announced.

Stuart Flannigan made a grand entrance with his wife and a young woman Wade assumed to be his daughter. The trio beelined for Sherry, beckoning for Wade to join them.

"Mrs. Kline." Flannigan shouted her name across the room, startling guests with the loud outburst.

Glancing around self-consciously, Sherry hurried over.

"Good evening, Mr. Flannigan. Caroline. And you must be Tiffany."

The young woman eyed the room with a bored expression. "Yeah. I'm Tiffany Flannigan."

"I hope you and your step—" Sherry corrected herself before referring to Flannigan's fifth wife as his daughter's stepmother since Caroline was closer in age to Tiffany than to Stuart. "I hope you both enjoyed your visit to the resort spa. It's one of the top-rated facilities in the world."

"Thank you for arranging it, Sherry." Caroline's demeanor was much more gracious than at last night's cocktail reception. "Orna, the aesthetician you recommended, was wonderful. She applied a special treatment that was less abrasive because I wanted to look my best tonight."

"You look amazing." Sherry's smile held genuine warmth. "I'm glad you selected the aquamarine dress. It picks up the blue in your eyes and highlights the golden tones of your tan."

Wade noticed the evening gown Caroline wore was much more tasteful than the too-tight black sequined dress she'd previously worn. She looked less like a high-class call girl and more like a wealthy housewife of some large metropolis.

"Antonio held a private showing for me in the resort's boutique after I finished at the spa. He served champagne and had models parade through in the dresses he thought would be best suited for my color palette. I'm a summer, by the way." Caroline twisted and turned so they could admire every angle.

"Zoey Foster, the resort owner, said Antonio studied design under Gianni Versace," Sherry stage whispered.

"Did you say Versace?" Tiffany no longer looked disinterested. "Can you schedule an appointment for me, too?"

A waiter circulating with drinks approached. He stood at a discreet distance and waited. Sherry lifted a glass of beer off the tray and handed it to Flannigan. "This is for you. It's a Sheffield."

His jaw dropped in surprise, then he lifted the glass in the air like a trophy. "I'm impressed, Mrs. Kline. How do you know Sheffield is my preferred drink? It's good stuff. They're one of the best beer producers in the UK."

"Sheffield does have the best brewery in Europe," Wade agreed.

Sherry handed a wine glass to Caroline. "This Chardonnay is produced locally and has earned several awards. Try it."

Caroline took a sip, her face relaxing into a pleasant smile which went all the way to her blue eyes. "Sweet, just the way I like it."

"Sonoma Valley Vintners produce exquisite wine. Most of the wineries are small and run by families, but there are a few celebrity-owned estates. Organic wine enthusiasts often tour this region because they offer over a hundred award-winning vintages." Sherry had obviously spent time with Steel Foster, who handled the resort's vineyard and winemaking operation. He'd given the same spiel to Wade earlier in the day.

Wade lifted the last two glasses of wine from the tray and handed one to Sherry. "What would you like to drink, Tiffany? I'll have the server bring something for you."

"Jack and Coke with an extra shot of Jack." She didn't even look at Wade as she dictated her order.

Like father, like daughter.

"It's against the law to serve alcohol to minors in the US," Sherry said casually. "I tried the raspberry lemonade at lunch. Perhaps you'd like that. Or maybe the mango iced tea?"

Wade expected Flannigan to override Sherry's suggestion, but he only frowned in disapproval at his daughter.

"Tiffany, you promised no more drinking," he scolded. "You're still on probation."

"Fine. I'll have *lemonade*." She exaggerated the word to convey her displeasure and wandered off into the throng of people.

Caroline raised her glass up to the light, examining the glimmer of the liquid. "I'd like to learn more about Sonoma Valley wines. This is my first visit to the area, and Stuart knows I love good wine." Caroline took a sip, swirling the liquid in her mouth before swallowing. "Chardonnay, Cabernet Sauvignon, and Pinot Noirs are among my favorites."

"The Sonoma Valley's Pinot Noir comes in different earthy flavors like berry and grape. I'll ask Steel Foster to send a bottle of each to your villa if you'd like," Sherry offered.

"Oh. Yes. That would be...nice." Caroline looked surprised, as if people weren't usually so thoughtful. "Do you think it would be possible to do a wine tour?"

"If anyone can make it happen, Steel can. Let me slip out and make those arrangements for you right now."

"Thank you, Sherry. That's kind of you."

Again, Sherry had used exactly the right tact to meet the needs of someone and bring out the best—or at least not the worst—in them. Caroline Flannigan certainly didn't *need* wine or facials. What the young woman needed was kindness and friendship.

Wade watched Sherry wend her way through the crowd and out of the room. He immediately felt her absence. When she wasn't with him, the warmth surrounding him disappeared.

"I'm impressed by the quality of the employees I've met,

especially Mrs. Kline." Flannigan wore a satisfied expression. "The selection of award winners seems appropriate. Well done, Briggs."

"Thank you." He exhaled, the tension gripping his body easing as Flannigan and his wife moved on. His muscles eased, and it was all because of Sherry. She was special. Caring and charming, strong and smart. Beautiful and desirable.

The guests took their dinner seats after enjoying an array of mouth-watering appetizers and cocktails. Wade had fixed it so that he and Sherry were seated at the same table, with a few seats between them just to be appropriate, yet still have her near. The conversation picked up as salads were served and continued throughout dinner. When the plates were removed, the tables cleared, and after-dinner aperitifs and coffee offered, the award ceremony commenced.

Lewis Quincy, one of the executives from the Australian office, served as host. He announced each recipient, who came up to the dais to receive their award from Flannigan who smiled into the camera like he was auditioning for a talent show, and then either returned to their seat or stood at the podium to say a few words

Flannigan's fears that the speeches would go on and on were unfounded. Most people uttered thanks to the significant people in their lives, proud and happy in their moment of achievement.

Soon, only two awards remained on the table.

Lewis clicked off his handheld microphone and sat down as Flannigan rose and marched to the podium. He tapped the microphone, sending feedback squawking over the sound system.

"Sorry about that." He tapped it a second time with the same results. Lewis hopped up and whispered some advice in his ear. Flannigan leaned back a bit and kept his hands in his pockets. "Let's try that again."

The audience laughed. Flannigan wasn't entirely a jerk, Wade realized. He had some degree of charisma that earned trust from employees. But Wade had seen another side of Flannigan—the entitled CEO who loved to wield his top executive power. He remembered how Sherry had so effectively handled Flannigan earlier. He had to do the same when he proposed his plan if he hoped for any chance at preventing jobs from being lost.

"This has been a banner year for Stallion." Flannagan plastered on a smile as fake as the eyelashes his wife was wearing. "Despite a record-breaking number of natural disaster claims filed in the US, profits are up by seven percent. The board is considering a number of strategies to minimize losses and ensure the ongoing success of Stallion as the premiere global insurance provider. We cannot make that happen without you." He cocked his head and stared into the camera as attendees applauded politely.

"Every year, Stallion recognizes its top performers with a week-long luxury vacation and a commemorative award." He gestured for Lewis to hand him the two final crystal awards, one twice as large as the other. "Our final recipient this evening is not only Employee of the Year for her local unit but is also being honored at the corporate level. Join me in congratulating Mrs. Sherry Kline, project manager with the Des Moines office and this year's top award winner."

Wade watched Sherry, emotions flicking across her face like a series of projector slides—shock, amazement, disbelief, excitement. The woman sitting next to her nudged Sherry, prodding her up and out of her chair. Her eyes darted around the room, coming to meet Wade's.

He stood up and began clapping. Others at the table rose,

adding their applause to his until a thunderous roar filled the room. He lifted his chin, urging her to claim her awards.

All eyes, including his, were on Sherry as she made her way to the dais. Flannigan clasped her fingers in a hearty handshake, then presented both awards to her.

"Thank you for your contributions to Stallion Protection Partners. In addition to these engraved awards, you will receive a bonus in the amount of twenty-five thousand dollars. On behalf of the board of directors and all the members of our company, congratulations!" Flannigan stepped to the side, allowing Sherry to access the microphone.

"Wow." She smiled tremulously, eyeing the awards, one clasped in each hand. "To say I'm overwhelmed would be an understatement. I've only been with Stallion a couple of years, but in that time, I've learned I work with an amazing group of people. Individually, each person brings their unique talents and abilities to the table, but only with strong leadership can those skill sets be transformed into teamwork and collaboration. My thanks to Arnold Bivens, who steers the ship in Des Moines, Marcia Wallace, vice-president of Midwest operations, and Wade Briggs, president of the North American division. I'd also like to extend my appreciation to Mr. Stuart Flannigan and Stallion's board of directors."

She blinked several times as another round of applause rang out.

"For some people, a job is just that. A job. A way to pay the bills and feed your family. Three years ago, I lost my husband unexpectedly. I had bills to pay and kids to feed so I went back to college. From there, I hired on with Stallion. While working, I rebuilt my life, found a way to move forward instead of holding on to the past, and have met some very special people."

Her eyes landed on Wade and stayed there, while all of his breath left his chest as if he'd run into a brick wall.

"I'm proud to work for a company that values its people. Thank you so much for this honor."

Applause followed her all the way back to the table. She slid gracefully into her seat and set the awards down. The women on either side of Sherry admired the trophies as people whispered congrats.

Lewis Quincy returned to the podium and announced there would be a fifteen-minute intermission so the room could be set up for the evening's entertainment, a local band quickly gaining international attention. Guests were encouraged to visit the bar, mingle, and return for a few hours of dancing.

When Lewis announced the name of the band, squeals and screeches sounded from a table near the front of the room.

"It sounds like Tiffany and her friends approve," Wade said to Sherry over the noise as people began leaving. "How did you manage to find a band with no advance notice?"

Sherry slumped back in her chair, content weariness vibing off her. "Zoey Foster knows someone who went to high school with the mom of the lead singer. She called in a favor and voila!"

"Well done, Mrs. Kline."

"Did you know about this?" she asked, pointing to her award, which looked like a flame made out of jade glass standing on a base.

"Of course. It's been difficult to keep the secret." He scooted his chair closer to hers. "What are you going to do with your bonus? Or is that rude to ask?"

She blushed, the color warming her pale cheeks. "I've no idea. Twenty-five thousand is a lot of money. I'm sure I can put it to good use somewhere."

He glanced around the room. "Are you going to stay and enjoy the band?"

"The music is not to my taste, but as long as Mr. Flannigan is happy, I think my job is done here. I think I'll call it a night."

"Need help carrying your awards back to your cottage?" Wade offered, not wanting the evening to be over yet.

"Yes, please." She handed him the larger award. "They're heavier than they look."

Wade and Sherry strolled out of the room, in step, heading toward the garden path leading toward the cottages. They paused when the clang of steel drums sounded in the distance.

Wade turned his head, trying to discover where the noise was emanating from. "Is there another event tonight?"

"Zoey told me there's some sort of Jamaican beach bash." Sherry made a face and laughed. "I suppose it's for the younger guests."

"Define young. To an eighty-year-old, fifty is young."

She shrugged. "They do say age is just a number."

"When was the last time you danced to the beat of a drum or laughed so hard you got the hiccups?"

Her eyes widened, but she didn't speak.

"I take it you get the hiccups when you laugh, too?" Wade grinned.

"No, but my daughter does."

He stopped on the path to face her. "I propose we crash this party and show the younger generation how we can move."

"Are you serious?" She laughed, tilting her head to meet his eyes.

"C'mon. It will be fun. Besides, you deserve some playtime."

She looked down at her outfit. "But what about these clothes? I wouldn't want the salt water or sand to ruin them."

"Let's take five minutes to drop off your awards and so you can change into something less formal."

A breeze off the ocean tossed a strand of hair across her face as she made a decision. "Maybe for a little while."

Her acceptance was like taking off from a stoplight in his Porsche. The joy and bliss of being pressed back in his seat, the thrill of the speed. He wasn't afraid of how fast he was connecting with Sherry. He was thrilled and wanted more.

Lots more.

Ten minutes later, they returned to the beach where the party was happening. Without thinking, Wade slipped his hand into hers. Flames of excitement sparked, and Sherry turned to look at him. The calm expression on her face warmed his heart.

They blended in with the crowd, dancing to a lively song, then another and another.

Sherry waved her hands in the air and wiggled her hips to the tune. Wade loved watching her move, each song releasing more of her inhibitions. He reached out to steady her when one of the other dancers accidentally bumped into her.

Sherry looked up into his face, her chest heaving from the exertion of dancing. Wade's hands tightened around her waist. Although she had regained her balance, he held on, unwilling to let go and break the delicate threads binding them in the moment.

"We should...head back." Sherry's words were a breathless whisper.

A gush of air rushed through his lungs and his fingers trembled as desire filled his body. Wade yearned to pull her into a tighter embrace but resisted, reminding himself she was off-limits.

"Or...we could stay for another music set," he suggested

to avoid returning to his empty villa. He realized this was the first time since his divorce that he was reluctant to be on his own. "Sherry, I—"

Her eyes twinkled as a joyful expression flickered across her face.

Oh, he wanted to tell her everything he was feeling, share the excitement and uncertainty of folding her in his arms. In that moment, he wanted more than a dance. He wanted her pressed up against him. He wanted to caress her soft skin with his lips. He wanted…no, he couldn't go there.

He was not going to spoil this moment with an ill-timed admission that he was falling for her.

"What were you about to say?" Her head tilted slightly to the side, and she looked so beautiful in the light of the full moon.

"I just wanted to say how nice these past few days have been. I've really enjoyed getting to know you." He purposely kept his tone and words light and informal.

"I've enjoyed these days as well, but I get the impression that's not what you were going to say."

"No. I was going to say how beautiful you look and how I love the reflection of the moon in your eyes, but I didn't want to scare you."

Sherry lifted her chin. "My, my, Mr. Briggs. You sure have a way with words. And don't worry about scaring me. I'm tougher than I look. Would you grant me the next dance?"

He'd do just about anything that would keep her in his company because, at this moment, he wanted to forget they were at a company function, forget he was essentially her boss, and forget the other hundred million obstacles preventing him from kissing her—because he wanted to kiss her.

He wanted that more than anything else in the world.

If only he were just as brave.

Chapter 9

*S*herry woke up slowly, rising through layers of wakefulness like a balloon carried on a breeze through billowy mounds of clouds until it burst into pure, radiant sunshine. Eyes still closed, she nestled into the softness of the pillow top mattress and then unfurled her arms into a wide, open stretch.

"What a wonderful dream," she murmured to an empty room.

She was slow dancing with a man, his hands low on her hips, her cheek pressed against a cotton dress shirt warmed by the man's body heat and scented with cologne and perspiration. Wherever they were, it was dark, the space illuminated by the glow of moonlight or maybe those pretty Japanese lanterns people hung on patios and decks. She didn't know and didn't really care...except that when she looked up, the man's face disappeared into shadow.

The effortless way they moved together in time to some vague romantic melody reminded her of dancing with John. After years together, they knew each other so well words weren't needed. Patterns and habits were etched deeply into the grain of their relationship, like names in a heart carved into a tree trunk.

The physical need to get closer to the man, to push away the fabric of his shirt so she could lay her cheek against his skin, and her impatience to feel his hands pull her closer was lightyears away from the comfortable, almost predictable lovemaking that came after twenty-three years of marriage. This hunger—this craving—was new and sharp and urgent. Like the impulse she'd been resisting to reach out and touch Wade. To run her fingers over the short, neat hair on the back of his neck. To loop her arm through his in a subtle claim of ownership. To lean back into the strength of his muscular chest.

Had she been dancing with John or Wade?

Did the dream reflect treasured memories of her past or sparkling hopes for a future she'd never considered? She sat up and wrapped her arms around her shins as she analyzed her reaction to the dream, the snowy white sheets a tangle around her waist.

She and John were high school sweethearts. They'd married right after graduation. He was the only man she ever dated and the only man she'd been intimate with. She loved the life they'd built together.

Eventually, after the grief of losing him, the memories had become more sweet than sad.

What she'd revealed in her award speech was true. She'd rebuilt her life and moved forward. The part about meeting some very special people—a special *person*—was a recent development. It had only happened a few days ago when she'd met Wade in person and got more acquainted during the shuttle ride from the airport to the resort.

Zoey Foster and Amy Denham, and even poor frazzled Kimberly, helped Sherry realize she'd been holding herself apart from people at work. She tried to be friendly and personable, but she'd been afraid to let down her guard. She didn't want pity or sympathy or special consideration because she was a widow.

Being on the receiving end of pity had been one of her biggest concerns about attending the award ceremony and one of the first false beliefs to be debunked. A few people got tongue-tied when they learned her husband had died, but most expressed sympathy and that was that.

Alison predicted the trip would be a significant milestone in confronting her fears and getting on with life. In just three days, Sherry had helped avert a disaster, impressed a temperamental executive, danced on the beach under tiki torches, and was developing a...friendship...with a smart, attractive, accomplished man who went to impressive lengths for the people he was responsible for. Even strangers, like Alex and the shuttle driver's mother.

Energized by the progress she was making and eager to see what the new day would bring, Sherry hopped out of bed. She crossed to the bathroom and caught her reflection. Alison, so thoughtful and caring, had tucked a pink satin nightshirt with the price tags still on it into her suitcase. The cool fabric skimmed Sherry's thighs, belly, and breasts, making her feel playful and sexy and vibrant. She smiled even as tears stung the backs of her eyes. She couldn't picture herself amidst the decadent luxury of the cottage wearing her faded Snoopy and Woodstock pajamas and was glad Alison had been so ruthless in her focus to make sure she had a good time.

After brushing her teeth, she padded out to the kitchen. Liquid gold sunshine had burned off most of the early morning haze, revealing the rich hues of the coastline. The intense green and brown of the stalwart trees, cliffs that were a muted collage of tan and gray, and the sapphire waves edged with white froth. She decided to order a big breakfast and enjoy it in front of the huge front window to savor the view. The friendly woman who took her phone order said the meal would be delivered shortly.

She wondered how Wade was starting his day. He didn't seem the type to sleep in, and she knew he was anxious to meet with Stuart Flannigan. Glancing at the microwave clock, a gasp escaped as she realized it was after nine. Even on the weekends, she was up and dressed by seven.

A bit unsettled by the break from her routine, she texted Alison.

Hi, honey. Time to chat?

Her phone buzzed, the display confirming the caller was her daughter.

"Hi, Mom." Alison's perky voice made Sherry homesick. Last night would have been even more meaningful if her children had been there. At least she had Wade to celebrate with.

"How's everything in Des Moines?" Sherry sank onto the beige suede sofa and curled her feet under her.

"A typical workday. Ridiculous traffic, a line out the door at Starbucks, and two of the bank tellers called out sick." Even when complaining, Alison sounded cheerful. "How is the resort? As gorgeous as the photos on their website? Are you relaxing and having fun? Tell me about last night. I can't wait to see your award."

Jumping in when Alison paused for breath, Sherry shared all the details. "The Silver Fox Resort is unbelievable, and the service has been impeccable. There were a few last-minute complications, and the executive assistant coordinating everything had to leave for a family emergency. I volunteered to help out—"

"Mom! You're not there to work," Alison interrupted.

"It wasn't a big deal, honey. Really," Sherry said. "Wade Briggs, the president of the North American division, helped out, and the staff at the resort went above and beyond to make sure the evening was perfect."

"Was it?"

"Was it what?" A trio of seagulls dive-bombed a fisherman on the beach and distracted Sherry.

"Perfect," Alison drawled.

"Aside from wishing you and your brother were there, it was pretty close." A bubble of excitement swelled in her chest. "All of the recipients were thrilled to receive their honors. The highpoint of the event was when the CEO from Stallion headquarters in Australia announced the corporate-wide Employee of the Year award winner." She paused expectantly.

"Was it someone you know?" Alison asked.

"You could say that." Sherry giggled, giving away the secret.

"No way!" Alison's exclamation was so loud Sherry had to pull the phone from her ear.

"Yes way!" They laughed together, then Sherry went on. "I got a second award and a $25,000 bonus. Wade knew the entire time we were working together on the reception and banquet and never said a thing."

"Wade?" Alison teased. "I'm assuming *Wade* is Mr. Briggs. Please don't tell me he's fat, bald, and closing in on retirement."

"He's not," Sherry assured her, picturing Wade's silver fox good looks. "He's about my age, divorced, two sons starting at the University of Colorado in the fall, and is a very nice man."

"Hmmm. Sounds like you two have a few things in common." Alison chuckled softly. "Sounds like you two should sneak away for a day of sailing or hiking or something."

"You can get that idea out of your head right now, young

lady." A trickle of regret coursed down Sherry's spine. "From what I can tell, Wade and I are the only people who didn't bring a guest along. We also work together and when his assistant had to leave, it made sense for me to step in. There's nothing more to it than that."

"Do you like him?" Alison persisted.

Sherry's first impulse was to deny her attraction, but she didn't. She sensed some connection with Wade, and he'd given her a few indicators he felt the same. Long, lingering looks. The invitation to attend the Jamaican beach party. Casual, not inappropriate touches, but the type of courtly gestures a man gave a woman on a date—cupping her elbow to steady her on the gravel path, draping her shawl around her shoulders, ordering another glass of wine when he noticed hers was empty.

"He's my boss. President of the North American division. He lives in Denver." Disappointment tugged at her heart. "I like him very much, but the timing and logistics are all wrong."

She expected Alison to come back with a pithy suggestion to go for it anyway, but she just murmured something that sounded like curious bemusement.

"Hmm. I am very proud of you, Mom. Dad would be, too." A rustling sound came over the phone, and then Alison was back on the line. "I have to go. I'll check in with you later. For now, you are under strict orders to not lift a finger unless they are wrapped around a glass of wine."

"Okay. Have a good day, honey." Sherry ended the call at the exact moment a tap sounded at her door.

Breakfast.

After thanking the server who set the tray on the glass-topped table near the sofa, Sherry drizzled warm syrup over a stack of fluffy pancakes and forked a bite into her mouth.

She decided to take her daughter's advice and make the most of her vacation. She'd earned it.

"I deserve it," she said in a firm voice.

She almost cringed at the words—the entitled statement sounded like something Caroline Flannigan might say—but it was the truth. She'd worked hard to keep body and soul together the past few years. She'd never splurge on a vacation at a high-end resort, but since this stay was paid in full by Stallion, it would be a sin to not indulge.

Speaking of indulging, her thoughts turned back to Wade and his scrumptious good looks, and a tingling sensation waltzed up her spine.

Chapter 10

*W*ade pounded out another mile on the treadmill in the resort's gym before allowing himself to call it quits. Up at five thirty after a sleepless night, he pulled on workout clothes and put himself through a grueling five-mile run, twenty minutes of weights, and another fifteen minutes of stretches.

His muscles trembled with exhaustion, but his mind was still a vortex of emotion: concern for his employees and his powerful attraction to Sherry that overshadowed everything else.

His ardent attraction concerned him the most.

While the company didn't have an official policy against dating coworkers, Wade knew workplace romances were potential landmines that could ruin lives and careers. That was especially true when the romance included a boss and subordinate. To avoid trouble, Wade didn't mix business and pleasure.

He didn't plan to compromise his ethics now, but the decision brought a truckload of regret. Sherry was an amazing woman, and they had so much in common. Not just their marital status and having mostly grown kids, but their values and priorities—a strong work ethic, commitment to family and friends, generosity, and kindness.

For weeks, he'd been obsessed with coming up with an alternative strategy to save jobs and minimize further losses for the company. He'd developed a solid plan but needed Flannigan to buy into the idea before presenting the radically different concept to the board. In the days leading up to the award ceremony, his sole focus had been tweaking and refining the proposal so Flannigan couldn't say no.

Now, his mind kept wandering from the proposal to Sherry. She filled his waking thoughts and nighttime dreams. He barely knew her, yet he could envision a future with her. Something in his gut warned him that letting Sherry walk away would be a huge mistake.

Frustrated with Flannigan's lack of commitment to employees, especially after the grandiose speech he'd given at the banquet last night, Wade had already considered the extreme decision to resign. Yet, leaving felt like abandoning people who needed him, thus the reason he hadn't made a final decision. He vowed to do everything in his power to persuade Flannigan to take a different course of action, but if Stallion insisted on selling off units when there was another viable option, he simply could not stay.

Finances weren't an issue; he had solid investments and had paid off his mortgage. Finding another job wouldn't be an issue either. Wade got two or three offers a month from competitors.

The question wasn't stay or go. The question was even more personal. Getting to know Sherry had raised new questions.

What did Wade want to do with the rest of his life?

The answer was easy—reconnect with his sons, make a

difference in the lives of others, explore the possibility of something real and lasting with Sherry.

The devil was, as the saying went, in the details.

Sherry had a life in Des Moines. She was devoted to her children and was building a successful career. He lived in Denver, and his sons would live nearby for the first time in three years.

"You're up early." A masculine voice interrupted his thoughts.

A tall, ruggedly attractive man Wade recognized as the resort's chef, Nate Keller, stepped onto the adjacent treadmill. Unlike Wade, who was slumped over the control panel wheezing in lungfuls of air and whose t-shirt was stained with sweat, Nate looked fresh and energized.

"Just working off some of those calories I took in last night." Wade grabbed the towel he'd draped over the treadmill's frame and blotted the sweat out of his eyes. "The food alone is worth a stay at the resort."

"Make sure you tell Zoey that. She's trying to get me to cut back on my hours so we can spend more time together." He fake-grimaced and chuckled. "We work together and go home together. I'm not sure how much more together we can be."

Wade understood Zoey's request. She was talking about *quality time*. Time without distractions and intrusions and interruptions. Moments shared exploring and experiencing, living and being in the moment.

He wanted that with Sherry. He wanted to get to know her. What movies she enjoyed. What items were on her bucket list. Her biggest fears. But first, he had to deal with Flannigan.

"Let me share a hard-learned lesson." Wade kept his tone light. "You don't regret those missed opportunities until they're gone. It's easy to assume there will always be time. I never anticipated being divorced and living thousands of miles from my kids. Grab hold of those special moments when they come along."

"Man, that's got to be rough." Nate gave him a quick sideways glance.

"It's hard not to beat myself up. I just don't want you to have the same regrets in ten or fifteen years." Wade wondered if Sherry dealt with any self-recriminations, wishing she'd spent more time with her husband or told him she loved him more often before losing him so suddenly.

He should consider himself lucky. Life was giving him a second chance to reconnect with Kip and Luke. Was it also offering him a second chance at love?

Love?

That was a serious word to already be tossing around, but Sherry Kline wasn't the kind of woman who indulged in casual affairs. There was no guarantee a relationship with her would end in happy ever after...but the potential sure as hell was there.

She was a forever kind of woman.

The question was what kind of man was he? Workaholic executive? Dedicated father? Committed husband?

"Have a good work out." Nate quickened his speed.

"Will do." Giving Nate a two-fingered salute, Wade tossed the towel in a convenient hamper and wondered if he could be all three.

Chapter 11

Sherry would never look at bees or honey the same, thanks to Steel Foster.

After her delicious breakfast and quick phone call with Alison, she'd showered and dressed in casual white jeans, a red and white striped blouse, and comfortable flats. She wasn't up for a hike, but a relaxing stroll through the resort's gardens to collect inspiration from the different plants and flowers for her organic beauty products before attending the honey tasting scheduled for later in the morning appealed to her. She'd added several notations to a small notebook, including suggestions offered by one of the resort's gardeners who was knowledgeable about the local flora. The gray-haired man recommended blending plants Sherry never would have mixed together, but he went a step further, presenting her with leaves and flowers from plants in the garden.

As Steel Foster continued his lecture about bees and honey production, she lifted her wrist to her nose, inhaling the faint aroma of white sage and lavender. She rubbed her fingers over her pulse point to reactivate the oil from the plants, pleased to recognize additional notes she hadn't identified before.

Genevieve, an accountant from Stallion's office in France, caught her eye and raised her brow in question.

"Tell you later," Sherry whispered.

She'd met the elegant Frenchwoman and her husband at last night's event. After a brief conversation about the resort's many amenities, Genevieve had invited Sherry to join her and several other women who were attending a honey tasting. Flattered, and happy to be included, she accepted.

They sat around a large rectangular table in a private room connected to the restaurant in the resort's main building. Floor to ceiling windows framed a spectacular view of the ocean and shore, but Steel Foster, the youngest of the Foster siblings and the resort's vintner, had no trouble keeping their attention.

Tall, attractive, and charismatic, he bantered easily with the women, sharing bits about the resort, his family, and the region. His passion for growing grapes showed in his enthusiastic explanation about the important role bees played in wine production.

"Healthy vines grow in an environment that includes other plants. While grapevines can self-pollinate, bees are essential for pollinating other crops and plants, which help regulate nitrogen levels and organic material in the soil. Maintaining a healthy ecosystem without relying on pesticides and chemicals produces a superior quality grape, which in turn produces better wine." Steel flashed a brilliant smile. "I'll bet you never guessed you owe that excellent glass of Chardonnay to a honeybee."

The women laughed and murmured agreement.

"Before I tell you about the hives here at the Silver Fox Resort Vineyard, let's go back a few thousand years." Steel lifted a jar containing a block of honeycomb sitting in a pool of golden liquid. "Historical records dating back to 2100 BC include references to honey. It has been used as a form of currency as recently as the eleventh century when German peasants paid feudal debts with honey and beeswax. While most commonly used as a natural sweetener, honey also has medicinal benefits and is a popular home remedy for burns and wounds."

He handed the jar to April, an insurance adjustor from the office in Atlanta, who sat closest to him, indicating she should pass it around as he spoke.

"Honey is made of water, minerals, and protein but it is seventy to eighty percent sugar. I won't share the specific process by which bees manufacture honey because you'd make a face and say, 'Ew!'"

Again, there was laughter and a few exaggerated exclamations.

"Far better to appreciate the final product." Steel pulled a tray of crystal syrup pitchers with silver levered tops in front of him, each labeled with a small tag and filled with honey that ranged in color from caramel brown to translucent amber. "What distinguishes each variety is the type of flower where the bee collects pollen. You may have heard of orange blossom honey or clover honey, but other varieties include acacia honey, chestnut honey, and sage honey. There are also different production techniques which is why you can select raw or pasteurized honey, whipped honey, and honeycomb."

"How do you tell the difference?" Genevieve asked.

"That is a very good question." Steel aimed his killer smile at the Frenchwoman, and Sherry noticed a faint blush color her cheeks.

Steel Foster was handsome and well dressed and knew how to work an audience, especially when it was all women. Sherry appreciated his masculine appeal, but he didn't set her

senses tingling like Wade did. Reflexively, she scanned the
bank of windows as if she might catch sight of him.

"Pasteurizing tends to homogenize the taste of honey, so
if you're looking for the best gastronomic experience, choose
raw, unfiltered honey. Be aware that varieties can vary in
texture, sweetness, and color. Medicinal benefits also vary.
Acacia honey, which is not sourced from the trees native to
Australia and Africa but the black locust tree—sometimes
referred to as the 'false acacia tree'—is high in antioxidants
believed to benefit heart health. Buckwheat honey is known
for its antibacterial properties. Manuka honey, a rare variety
produced in New Zealand from the tea tree bush, has
actually been approved by the FDA to treat wounds."

"My mom always gave us a spoonful of wildflower honey
when we had a cough," April said. "It tasted much better than
menthol cough drops." She scrunched her nose to show her
dislike.

"Before we start sampling the honey, look at the notecard
in front of you." Steel held up a white rectangle a bit larger
than an index card. "The Pfund scale is a guide used in the
industry to classify color. Intensity ranges from water white
to dark amber. Keep in mind that color is not indicative of
quality. It's simply one feature that differs across varieties."

Genevieve leaned over to Sherry. "I never knew honey
was so fascinating."

"Steel Foster could make wet paint fascinating," she
whispered back, covering her mouth to hide her laughter.

"Another characteristic that defines honey is the texture."
Steel lifted the dispensers at each end of the tray and swirled
them slowly. "Viscosity ranges from thick and gritty to a
thin, silky consistency. There are pencils and checklists
around the table. Help yourself, and then we'll start the
honey tasting."

For the next forty minutes, Sherry and the others

sampled half a dozen honey varieties, comparing notes on the flavor profiles, debating whether the Sourwood honey was more buttery or spicy, and agreeing unanimously that the macadamia nut honey was the best of the lot.

Steel concluded the tasting with an invitation to visit the apiary. "The bee yard is where we keep the hives. Jonah Masters is our resident beekeeper. He works with Sarah Decklin, our culinary specialist, who develops recipes and food products made from locally sourced ingredients, including our honey. You can purchase some of these items in the gift shop."

None of the women were interested in touring the hives, many citing fears of being stung, even though Steel assured them protective gear was available.

"No need to interrupt the worker bees," April said. "I'm sure I'm not the only one with plans to grab a jar or three of Silver Fox honey to take home. You're going to need to restock after the Stallion ladies clear the shelves."

"I hope you enjoyed learning more about our honey." Steel seemed to sense the group was ready to break up. "There are several dishes on the menu made with honey from our Silver Fox Resort hives. My personal favorites are the whipped feta drizzled with honey and the ginger-honey salmon."

"Oh, that does sound yummy. Thank you for today," Sherry said.

"Anytime." Steel gave her one of his character-defining friendly smiles. She might have swooned if she hadn't already seen Wade's smile.

She turned and followed the line of women exiting the private space into the dining room. More than half of the tables were already occupied by the lunch crowd. Her eyes were drawn to a two-top in a corner where Wade sat across from Stuart Flannigan.

Wade leaned forward in his chair, forearms resting on the edge of the table, brows furrowed, his mouth turned down. The CEO slumped casually in his chair, one ankle resting on his knee, fingers curled around a crystal tumbler. Flannigan ignored the blue folder Wade prodded across the table, instead rudely scanning the dining room.

Sherry's shoulders hunched in sympathetic apprehension, interpreting the tension in Wade's defensive posture. How could Flannigan sit there like Wade was making a sales pitch for something as mundane as toilet paper when he was proposing an idea that could save jobs and, eventually, turn a profit for the company?

Genevieve laid a hand on Sherry's arm. "Would you like to have lunch with us?" Three other women, including April, stood nearby.

Before she could answer, Wade shot out of his seat. Flannigan said something loud enough to turn heads but not clear enough for Sherry to make out the words. She watched Wade stalk out of the dining room, the blue folder crushed in his fist.

"Um…" She stammered, wanting to say yes in order to spend more time with her new acquaintances, yet yearning to follow Wade.

"Go see to Mr. Briggs. He's your special friend, no?" Genevieve's accent became more pronounced with her husky whisper. "He needs you."

"We're not…he's just…" Sherry felt an embarrassed flush heat her face.

"Trust me," Genevieve said, curving her arm around Sherry for a quick hug. "I am French. *Je sais pour l'amour.* Last night, I saw how he looked at you when your attention was elsewhere. It's the same way you stare at him when you think no one is watching."

Her cheeks heated to the point of burning.

"La vie est une fleur dont l'amour est le miel." Genevieve's crimson lips quirked into a tiny smile when Sherry shook her head, revealing she didn't understand. "A timely quote from Victor Hugo. 'Life is a flower, of which love is the honey.'"

Sherry burst into laughter. No matter what Genevieve thought, she and Wade were friends. There was nothing inappropriate about lending an ear to a friend in need.

Too bad she didn't entirely believe a simple friendship was the extent of her feelings for her sexy boss.

Chapter 12

"*S*tuart Flannigan is a horse's—"

"Wade! Wait up."

No one except Sherry Kline could put the brakes on his rant about Stallion's self-absorbed, self-centered, self-ish CEO. His fury diminished just enough that he was able to draw in a shaky breath and compose himself by the time Sherry crossed the lobby to stand in front of him.

"I saw you talking to Mr. Flannigan." Her brows dipped in a vee over eyes dark with worry. "Can I assume he didn't like your proposal?"

"I don't want to talk about it here." He looked around. Although there were no Stallion employees he recognized within earshot, any of the individuals walking past could be the spouse or guest of an employee. He didn't need his harsh, angry words being repeated.

"Let's take a walk on the beach," Sherry suggested. "It's private, and walking will burn off some of the adrenaline pumping through you right now."

"I need to swing by my villa and change out of this

monkey suit." Wade loosened his tie and released the top button of his starched blue dress shirt.

A performing monkey in Flannigan's circus was an apt description.

Grinding his teeth to keep his rage in check, Wade waved a hand, inviting Sherry to lead the way out.

They remained silent as they walked down the path side by side. The sun sat high in the sky but did little to warm the brisk wind off the ocean. When they arrived at his villa, Sherry dropped into one of the chairs on the small porch.

"Be right back," Wade growled.

"Take your time." She looked up at him with steady eyes.

"Aren't you signed up for horseback riding or a pottery class or..." He trailed off, his mind devoid of any of the activities he'd reviewed on Kimberly's list.

"I was reluctant to commit." Her shrug revealed a tinge of embarrassment. "Kimberly said I could decide when I got here."

"I don't want to keep you..." He regretted exposing Sherry to the fallout of his conversation with Flannigan.

"Wade, it's obvious you're upset. You shared enough that I can guess why." Her gaze dropped to the porch's plank flooring, then lifted. "If you want to be alone, I'll go. If you need a friend to sympathize, I'll listen. If you want to get drunk, I'll make sure you don't do anything stupid."

He wanted a CEO who cared about people instead of a high seven-figure bonus. The odds of that were in the single digit range; same as the odds he stood a chance at something more with Sherry.

Unable to speak, he jerked a nod, unlocked the door, and went in to change.

Flannigan's rejection of his proposal meant good, hard-working people like Sherry would soon be out of a job or, if they were lucky, be absorbed into the machinery of a competitor. They'd lose seniority, benefits, vacation time, and probably have to take a pay cut.

He unbuttoned his dress shirt with impatient fingers, sending one of the buttons arcing through the air. He flung his pants and suit coat over the nearest chair.

"Damn it!"

He shrugged out of his shirt, rolled it into a ball, and flung the wadded garment into the corner. It fluttered into a heap before the fabric brushed the wall.

In his socks and boxers, he strode to the bathroom, cranked the cold water, and tossed handfuls onto his burning face.

Sherry was right. Anger and adrenaline were surging through his body, making it hard to think clearly. Flannigan had forced him to perform his entire song and dance, smirking the whole time as if audience to a six-year-old performing "Swan Lake." The jerk.

Trite, but so entertaining.

He needed to calm down, vent his frustration, restore his equilibrium so he could think rationally. There had to be some way to prevent the company from selling off units, including Des Moines, as Flannigan intended.

"Wade? Are you okay?" Sherry called out from just inside the front door.

He peeked through the half-open bathroom door, emotion rushing through his arteries, into his capillaries, and back to his heart via his veins. The concern on her face was enough to soothe some of the negativity choking him.

"Just cooling off," he called. "I'll be out in five."

"The sky is clouding up out toward the horizon. If you want to walk, we should leave now." The door clicked shut softly as she retreated back to the porch.

Wade braced his hands on the edge of the sink and stared at his reflection in the mirror. God, he was getting old. He was almost entirely gray, lines were permanently etched at the corners of his eyes, and the skin on his neck wasn't as tight as it had been even five years ago. He was grateful he didn't yet have hair sprouting from his nose and ears, but the stress of the past few months hadn't done him any favors. He pulled the skin down under one eye, examining the sclera which was shot through with a few tiny red vessels.

His head fell forward, shoulders hunching under the oppressive burden of saving his employees. He refused to take no for an answer. While other executives might shrug and justify walking away by telling themselves they'd tried, it wasn't enough for Wade. He doubted his boss had heard a third of what he'd said, the man's eyes continually surveying the dining room as if on the outlook for a more entertaining lunch partner.

Impotent rage boiled in his veins again. He closed his eyes and pictured Sherry accepting her award last night. He remembered the sheen of tears as she explained her position with Stallion was more than a job, it had enabled her to rebuild her life after the loss that devastated her family. Her fervent words echoed in his mind, cooling his fevered blood.

If Sherry could figure a way out from the depths of despair, he could figure out a way to convince Flannigan.

Right now, though, he needed to clear his head and come at the problem from a different angle. Sherry had proven useful in resolving the last-minute problems related to the award ceremony. Maybe she could offer a different perspective that would enable him to get through to Flannigan.

He pulled on jeans, a lightweight navy pullover, and tennis shoes. Determined to make the most of the beach walk with Sherry, he shoved Flannigan out of his thoughts. Inhaling a calming breath, he placed his wallet and keycard in his back pocket and slipped on sunglasses.

Wade opened the front door. "Ready?"

She nodded, her features smooth and unconcerned, conveying trust and confidence. Her expression further decompressed his pent-up frustration. She knew what was at stake. She understood the implications if company units were sold off. She also comprehended how highly unlikely it would be for Flannigan to make an altruistic decision.

The odds were against them, yet not so much as a single line marred her brow. Without a word, she communicated empathy and understanding. She believed in him. Believed he would do everything possible to prevent her and her coworkers from losing their jobs and facing uncertainty. Yet she also knew life wasn't fair and what mattered most could be ripped away in seconds.

How could she remain calm and composed when the job and stability she'd labored so courageously to secure for herself and her kids was at risk of disappearing?

Because she'd already bounced back once.

From a loss that was a thousand times more devastating than being downsized, laid off, or reassigned.

The last of his anger dissipated, a startling realization taking shape at the edge of his consciousness. Vague, ephemeral, but slowly coming into focus.

"Let's walk," he said, slipping his hand under Sherry's elbow as they headed for a paved trail that ran parallel to the ocean's edge.

Silence stretched between them as they strolled through patches of sunshine and shadow. When the resort was no longer visible behind them, Sherry spoke.

"What did Mr. Flannigan say?"

"Nothing." Wade dropped his hand, allowing a gap to form between him and Sherry. "He barely paid attention. When I asked that he consider my proposal, he laughed."

"That's disappointing." Sherry matched his pace as he slowed.

"That's irresponsible," he scoffed.

"Corporations don't make decisions based on an approval rating." Her tone was annoyingly pragmatic. "Most companies operate on the basis that their first obligation is to shareholders. Stallion is no different than any other for-profit business."

"Are you telling me you believe the bottom line is more important than people?" He stopped and stared in disbelief.

"Of course not." Sherry looped her arm through his and tugged him along the trail. "I'm suggesting you stop making this personal. That might make it easier for you to talk to Mr. Flannigan without putting him on the defensive. I know you disagree with the recommendation to sell off units, but it's a practical decision."

"My plan is equally practical. It just requires more time," he argued, his tone sharper than he intended. "Sorry. I don't mean to take my anger out on you. It's just...you sound like Flannigan."

"You're emotionally invested in the outcome of this situation. You're equating the final decision as win or lose, failure or success." She leveled a gentle smile at him. "That's what makes you an outstanding leader and corporate president. You care about your people."

He did care about his employees. He wanted them to feel valued and secure in their jobs. His feelings for one employee—Sherry—were expanding into something far more meaningful. Was it possible those feelings were clouding his judgment?

The vague notion in his head snapped into place. His feelings for Sherry weren't complicating the situation—they were reminding him he had his own priorities. After his divorce, when Juliet took the boys and moved across the country, he'd lost a part of himself. He'd stayed in Colorado at first because he cherished his carefully crafted career. Working was at the core of who he was. Months went by before he realized he was missing out on a relationship with his sons. By then, the poison seed had already been planted, and his sons had already grown distant.

Yes, trying to save his employees' jobs was a valiant effort, but people could find other, maybe even better, jobs, but family and loved ones weren't replaceable.

Sherry was putting things into perspective.

"People are just one of many assets on a spreadsheet to Mr. Flannigan. You're expecting him to share your values when his primary motivator is profit. If you want to convince him to not cut jobs or sell off units costing Stallion money, you have to appeal to what matters most to him, not yourself."

Sherry's advice was so logical and concise, Wade wanted to slap his hand to his forehead for not seeing it sooner.

She was right. One hundred percent spot on.

This was personal. Nothing would change that for Wade. He couldn't relegate employees—people like Sherry and Kimberly who needed secure jobs in order to deal with bigger issues like death and illness—into a column on a profit and loss statement. But Sherry's observations about how he was approaching Flannigan were accurate.

Flannigan would not be persuaded by an argument that focused on the human element. He might, however, be swayed to change his recommendation to the board if Wade could prove retaining employees would yield a higher profit.

A renewed sense of optimism filled Wade, spurring him to twirl Sherry into his arms.

"Where were you six weeks ago?" He clasped her against his chest, his body registering soft curves and sweet heat. He pulled her in closer. "You gave me exactly what I need, Mrs. Kline."

The sound of those last two words dropkicked Wade back to reality. He released Sherry so quickly she stumbled before regaining her balance.

"I'm sorry. I don't know what I was thinking. Grabbing you like that was inappropriate. I should go. Rework my…" he sputtered. "I'm sorry, Sherry."

Her blue eyes widened with hurt, red embarrassment coloring her cheeks, reinforcing his error.

"Mr. Briggs. I—"

"No. Don't say it. I was in the wrong. Again, I apologize. It will not happen again."

"I see." She took a step back, her words heavy as if it took extra effort to squeeze them past her vocal cords. "You should go. Mr. and Mrs. Flannigan are scheduled to fly out the day after tomorrow. You don't have much time if you want a second chance to speak with him before he leaves."

She wheeled around and walked in the opposite direction.

Wade battled the impulse to go after Sherry and apologize for his hasty words. However, if he did catch up with her, he might not be able to resist kissing her and expressing how he really felt.

Instead, he forced himself to return to his villa where he stared at a blank page on his laptop, wondering where he'd gone wrong. Not with Flannigan, but with Sherry.

After an unproductive hour or so, he set his laptop aside, stood, and paced to the window, mulling over the thoughts cycling through his brain.

Four days ago, he'd been worried about saving hundreds of jobs. Now, the job that mattered most was Sherry's.

Three days ago, he realized how special Sherry was and

how much he wanted to spend all of his time with her. Yet, he didn't want to scare her off.

Two days ago, he had shuffled his goals and redefined his priorities. Now, his personal life and his professional obligations were a muddy, contradictory mess.

It wasn't that his job and commitment to his employees no longer mattered. It was just that Sherry was coming to matter *more*.

He needed to ground himself. Quit getting distracted. Remind himself again of who and what were most important in his life.

He grabbed his cell phone and a beer from the fridge and went out to the porch. He screwed off the lid, gulped down a swallow, and took in the setting sun for a moment before dialing the phone.

"Hey, Kip. It's your dad. Is your brother around?" Wade propped his bare feet on the porch rail and crossed them at the ankle. "Great. Put the phone on speaker."

A pause as Kip yelled something that came through the phone garbled.

"Luke's coming. Is everything okay?"

"Yep. A-okay." Wade took another sip from the bottle. "I was thinking about you and Luke and wanted to hear about your day."

"Cool. Here's Luke."

"Hi, Dad. What's wrong?"

"Nothing's wrong, son. I just wanted to hear your voice."

Note to self: Make sure to call the boys for no other reason than to say hello.

Chapter 13

"My trees look like party hats." April, the insurance adjustor from Atlanta and one of Sherry's new girlfriends, perched on her stool, green paint dripping off the paintbrush she held in one hand.

Genevieve bent to examine April's canvas and gave an elegant snicker. "*Oui.* But the shape is correct. My *arbres* look like starfish."

Sherry leaned back with a critical eye. Her landscape wasn't half bad. The pine trees looked like pine trees, the waves looked like waves, and the yellow ball in a swath of blue looked like a sun. She carefully dipped her brush into a daub of white acrylic paint, deciding where to add a highlight as suggested by Penny, the painting instructor.

"What do you think of mine?" Caroline Flannigan, seated at the easel next to Sherry, frowned at her canvas, her forehead smooth and unlined, undoubtedly a result of Botox injections. The wide apron barely covered her generous bustline, but she seemed unbothered by the splashes of paint staining her designer sundress.

Sherry was still trying to grasp why Caroline had signed

up for the painting class. Then again, her impression of Caroline had changed over the past few days. Gone was the brazen, insecure CEO's wife who flaunted her privilege and wealth. The woman sitting next to her today was much more subtle in her appearance and less abrasive to those around her. It seemed like she was trying to fit in, trying to find her place.

"It's the best of the bunch." Sherry's compliment was sincere. The young woman had a flair for color and composition, and the painting rivaled those adorning the studio walls.

"Truly?" Caroline's eyes narrowed.

"I always say what I mean. I value honesty, don't you?" Sherry glanced between Caroline and her talented artwork.

"If you're having trouble"—Penny returned to the front of the room and drew her and Caroline's attention—"use one of the photographs for inspiration. Turn it upside down and focus on the shapes and colors instead of trying to replicate what you see outside the window."

The slim sixtyish woman with leathery skin, a long gray braid, and faded blue eyes positioned a two-by-three-foot photo of the shoreline upside down on an easel. "Sometimes reframing what you see gives you the perspective you need."

The comment resonated with Sherry but for a different reason.

Still stinging from Wade's abrupt retreat yesterday, she'd spent the afternoon and evening avoiding him by having an early dinner with Genevieve and her husband at the resort's main restaurant and then accepting April's invitation to go into town to a local tavern that offered live entertainment and karaoke. Two glasses of Chardonnay gave her courage to get on stage with April and two other women—wives of Stallion award winners from Seattle and Detroit—for a comical rendition of Cyndie Lauper's "Girls Just Wanna Have Fun."

For a few hours, she'd forgotten about Wade, her growing attraction to him, and the potential job crisis. It felt good to laugh and put herself out there, the crowd's raucous shouts and applause rewarding their efforts. She made a silent vow to find a karaoke place in Des Moines and drag Alison and Claire out for a night of fun.

Back at her cottage, she'd struggled to hold on to the buoyant feelings. As she lay alone in the dark, she longed for someone to curl up against. She missed the haven of strong arms and husky, intimate promises that caused her skin to prickle with anticipation. She'd proven how strong she was, but Wade made her realize how lonely life had become.

When she'd called Alison that morning, her daughter again suggested Sherry hang out with her single boss, but the idea of dating and being with another man felt like a betrayal of her wedding vows. John had been everything to her, but was it realistic—was it fair?—to remain committed to a memory?

She'd never questioned her decision to avoid romance until meeting Wade. He made her feel things and want things —an intimate connection, physical touch, a special person to share new experiences and adventures with.

Rebuilding her life had changed her.

This trip proved that.

She was more confident. More independent. More resourceful. More courageous. If she reframed the situation with Wade, it wasn't that he'd rejected her. No, he'd reminded her she was a desirable woman, ready for a relationship with the right man.

Too bad that man couldn't be him.

"Your mind wanders again, *mon amie*." Genevieve approached and untied the denim apron protecting her clothing and draped it over her stool. "April and I have abandoned the idea of recreating Monet's visual mastery. Finish up and then join us at the pool. Caroline, you are invited as well. We plan to order a light lunch, spend a few hours soaking up the sunshine, and then decide what to do for dinner. Mike and Priscilla McMann, that delightful couple from Dallas, heard about a wonderful restaurant in town. I think they are making reservations for us."

"As long as it isn't the tavern." Sherry laughed softly. "Not unless you're up for burgers and karaoke."

"Kara-what?" Genevieve's thin brows lifted in confusion.

"It's where you get up in front of a crowd and sing along to recorded music." Sherry giggled at the look of horror crisscrossing Genevieve's face. "It's some people's idea of fun."

"Don't deny you had a good time," April chided as she hung her apron on a hook. "We just picked the wrong tune. We should have done 'Be My Baby' by the Ronettes."

Sherry groaned. "That song was performed three times. I couldn't get it out of my head last night. Next time, I'm going with 'Tequila.' It has one word."

"You're no fun." April grimaced in mock disapproval.

"Sherry is rediscovering her joie de vivre." Genevieve cupped Sherry's face and lightly kissed each cheek. "She enjoys *piendre*, painting. She will find new pursuits that fulfill *le coeur*."

Sherry had already created space in her heart by pushing aside fear.

For a fleeting moment, she thought Wade might help her fill the empty places. Regret burned the back of her throat.

"Go." Sherry made a shooing motion to urge April and Genevieve on their way. "Let me finish my painting. I'll join you for lunch in half an hour or so."

Caroline declined the pool invitation, explaining she'd

agreed to meet Stuart and Tiffany for an afternoon sailing excursion with one of her husband's American associates from nearby San Francisco.

"I must go," Caroline fussed. "Penny, will you see that my canvas is delivered to our villa?"

Penny assured her the request would be handled. Instead of Caroline haughtily walking off like she'd done to Sherry in the past, Caroline paused to thank the instructor for her time and vowed to tell her friends about Penny's gallery website. Mumbling something about being late, she set her apron on her stool and rushed out the door.

Penny, alone in the studio with Sherry, offered a few more tips until Sherry was satisfied with her work.

As she washed the acrylic paint from her hands, she wondered if Wade had had another opportunity to speak with Stuart Flannigan. He'd reviewed his proposal with her; it was solid. The arrogant CEO's refusal to hear out one of his highest-ranking executives bothered her. Not just because of the impact on her and her coworkers, but because narrow-minded leadership ultimately jeopardized the success of the corporation, no matter how big or small the business was. Stuart Flannigan had gotten away with biased decision-making so far, but she feared eventually he'd make a bad decision with enormous ripple effects there was no recovering from.

She said her goodbyes to Penny and made her way from the studio to her cottage. As she rambled along, she couldn't resist looking around for Wade. Was he still revising his pitch, or had he decided to take advantage of the break from work? The resort offered so many activities and amenities there was no way a visitor could experience all of them in just seven days. Even a month would be insufficient to attend all the offered classes. Plus, the California coastline was breathtaking, and it reminded Sherry how little of the world she'd experienced. Her and John's bucket list—now *her* bucket list—included Greece, Paris, Rome, New York City, Alaska, and the Grand Canyon.

Now that she'd ventured outside of Iowa, maybe she should schedule a trip to one of those other destinations. She could invite Alison or Tyler, join a tour group, or if worse came to worst, make the trip alone. That idea held little appeal. Not because she was scared to travel by herself but because life was better when shared with someone special.

Someone like—she shut down the thought but wasn't fast enough—*Wade.*

Her boss who was off-limits and who had made that crystal clear yesterday.

Keying the cottage door open, Sherry sighed. It was no good trying to ignore Wade and the feelings he stirred. With time, she'd get past this infatuation, this obsession. The best she could do now was stay busy and avoid him.

She eyed the teal-blue bathing suit with the skirted bottom and matching sarong. She'd sworn she wouldn't wear something so...so revealing. Alison might be pleased to hear she'd dared to wear it to the pool. But she refused to admit to anyone, except herself, she wore it in hopes Wade might wander by and get an eyeful.

Chapter 14

$\mathcal{W}$ade sat at the bar in The Olive Branch, savoring a dry martini. He'd considered ordering a glass of Chardonnay, but the sweet taste of crisp apples reminded him of Sherry, and he was doing his best to ignore his feelings.

Not wanting to run into her at the resort restaurant, he'd asked Amy Denham to recommend a place in town. She suggested this small, upscale bistro that boasted a tiny farm-to-table menu. All of the tables were occupied when Wade arrived except one reserved for a party of six. He didn't mind sitting at the bar. It afforded a good view of the open kitchen where the chef, Dominic Dupree, and two sous chefs prepared the food.

Wade recognized a few faces, Stallion employees who'd also ventured into town for dinner. He nodded politely, then returned to his drink. Rumor had it that misery loved company, but he doubted anyone would appreciate his contemplative state.

The door at the front of the restaurant opened, admitting a large group, happily chatting amongst themselves. More

Stallion folks, including the couple from France—Genevieve and Rupert, if he remembered correctly—Mike McMann and his wife, and…oh, no…

His heart rocketed to his throat then dropped like a lead weight to his knees. God, she looked amazing. She must have spent the day out in the sun because her skin glowed a rosy gold. Her hair, pulled up in a sleek knot, gleamed like strands of silk. She wore a linen blazer over a white dress, and both looked stylish but modest.

A thrill of possessive pleasure zinged through him. He had no claim on Sherry's affections, but at least she wasn't flaunting herself in front of other men like Juliet had done. Just a glance was sufficient to see the difference between the two women. Juliet would have worn something sheer and exposed as much flesh as possible because the narcissistic woman needed attention and ego strokes, which he assumed was what eventually led to her infidelity. Alternately, Sherry carried herself with the innate assurance of a woman confident and comfortable with herself.

"Hey, Wade." Mike crossed through the restaurant, clapping Wade on the shoulder. "Didn't expect to see you here. I thought you'd be having dinner with Flannigan and the other suits."

"You mean Quincy, Danvers, and Oldstein?" Wade named the three ranking executives from Australia also in attendance at the resort.

"Yeah. I know the rest of us are indulging in a well-earned vacation, but I assumed the top dogs would be meeting to discuss whatever it is top dogs discuss."

Wade narrowed his eyes, trying to read into Mike's comment. Was the Texan implying he knew something about possible job cuts or was it a simple statement? Based on the man's relaxed smile and casual posture, it was the latter.

"The North American division organized this year's

event. Since the cocktail reception and banquet are wrapped up, I'm on vacation like everyone else."

"Nice." Mike nodded approval. "It's been a tough year for some of our units. They say trouble rolls downhill, but I know a rising tide spills over, poisoning the waters for everyone. I hope you get a chance to decompress and relax. Say…" Mike looked over at his wife and gestured toward Wade. When she nodded, he went on. "April was supposed to be our sixth for dinner, but her husband got back early from his deep-sea fishing expedition, and they decided to dine at the resort. We have an extra place if you'd care to join us."

Wade peered past Mike, his gaze colliding with Sherry's. She gave him a tiny smile, and that was all the encouragement he needed. He'd been a jerk yesterday, thrusting her away as if she'd scorched him, but their hug was more than a simple embrace between friends. Holding her in his arms, the warmth of her skin leeching through the thin layers of cloth separating them, her unique scent imprinting itself on his memory—everything combined to create a powerful need for all of her. Her touch, her trust, her future, her affection.

Maybe once the situation with Flannigan was resolved—Sherry's termination or his own resignation—they could explore the possibility of a relationship because the just-friends label was too limiting.

"Yes," Wade said before he realized the word was on his lips.

"This is my wife, Priscilla, and you already know Sherry." Mike flicked his gaze between them.

"Hello." Wade nodded, afraid to say more.

Dinner with two other couples meant he and Sherry would be paired off. The company of four other adults also meant there would be no chance at any impropriety. For the first time all day, he felt his shoulders drop and the tension leave his body.

"Mr. McMann?" The hostess, a youngish woman with short black hair and green eyes, held a bundle of silverware wrapped in napkins, a stack of hand-written menus tucked under one elbow. "Your table is ready."

The group followed the hostess, settling into seats and ordering two bottles of wine as a server delivered a charcuterie board and small plates. The men sat next to each other, allowing the women to select the seats on the other side of the round table, an arrangement that allowed Wade to watch Sherry unobtrusively. She appeared relaxed among her newfound friends, which triggered a jab of jealousy and escalated his simmering need to know everything there was to know about Sherry. The task of staying neutral toward her was becoming impossible.

Excellent wine and a delicious meal, plus the company of educated, well-traveled, witty acquaintances, smoothed the underlying awkwardness until Wade and Sherry were talking and laughing with the other four. He discovered she had a droll sense of humor, and while she never made fun of others, she had a way of expressing herself that made it clear she wasn't naïve. In fact, she was quite astute. The way she'd handled Flannigan's ego and his wife's need for attention proved that.

When the others launched into a conversation in French, Wade leaned closer to Sherry.

"I'm sorry about yesterday," he said in a low tone. "I overreacted. It was an impulsive gesture. I hope I didn't make you uncomfortable."

She held his gaze, her expression unreadable. Her eyes dropped to the table for a moment, her lashes hiding her reaction. When she glanced back up, his heart and groin tightened simultaneously at the emotion whirling in the blue depths.

"I was only uncomfortable when you decided the action inappropriate." Her words were barely audible. "I liked being in your arms, Wade. I wasn't embarrassed or ashamed."

"Ashamed? You can't...you shouldn't..." How did this woman undo him with seven simple words?

"John was my first and only, so this attraction thing is all so new. I don't know how to pretend I don't like you. I don't *want* to pretend, especially after learning the hard way there are no guarantees we'll get another chance." She folded her hands on the table but kept her eyes locked on his. "If being coworkers is the problem, maybe it's me who should look for another job."

She reached out and touched his leg underneath the table. She was inviting him to take a leap of faith, a jump she'd already made.

"I'm flattered, Sherry, that you're willing to give up your job for me, but don't do it. You need your job."

Pain creased her face, and she slowly withdrew her hand. "I wouldn't be quitting for you, Wade."

Confusion joined the mix of regret and astonishment dulling Wade's thoughts. "No?"

"I talked to my daughter this afternoon." Sherry's tone and body language were stilted. "She asked about the bonus I got along with the corporate Employee of the Year award. We did some calculations, and it's enough to fully launch my small business. I can make a living selling organic bath and beauty products."

"I thought creating soaps and stuff was just a hobby." He scrubbed a hand across his chin. If Sherry no longer worked for Stallion, that changed everything.

"Many lucrative small businesses begin as hobbies," she replied with a defensive edge to the words. "The demand for my products has picked up. Alison and I believe we can make it work."

"Oh, Sherry." Wade laughed, relief and hope unfurling deep inside. "I didn't mean to insult you. I'm just…surprised." He fumbled around under the table until he found her hand and squeezed it tight. "There's a small shop down the street that specializes in similar products. How about if we visit tomorrow to start collecting information on how to turn your hobby into a dream come true?"

His outburst attracted the attention of their dinner mates. "What are you two up to with all this whispering?"

Sherry turned in her seat. "Wade is going to give me some advice on how to turn my hobby into a business. I make skin care products, and there is a shop in town that sells similar items."

"So, we'll visit tomorrow?" Wade waited for her answer.

Sherry blushed and twined her fingers with his, eyes misting as hopeful pleasure filled her. She turned back to him. "I'd love to."

Chapter 15

*S*herry wished the trip back to the resort from town would never end. Wade sat next to her in the hotel shuttle, his thigh pressing lightly against hers, the casual connection belying her intimate thoughts. As Alex navigated, the group continued to exchange anecdotes and stories, cementing their friendship.

For the first time since John died, Sherry felt a keen sense of belonging. Genevieve was quickly becoming a dear confidante, even inviting Sherry to visit their country house outside of Paris. Mike McMann's boisterous country boy persona was the complete opposite of Priscilla's genteel southern accent and demeanor, making them an interesting contradiction. Married for twenty-three years with six children between twelve and twenty, their love and dedication shone through, leaving no doubt their differences did not detract from the strength of their union. Like Genevieve, Priscilla had encouraged Sherry to call on them if and when she got to Dallas.

"Here you go, folks." Alex steered the shuttle to a smooth

stop in front of the main resort building, outdoor lighting illuminating the architecture. "Glad everyone enjoyed their visit into town."

Sherry and Wade waited until the others had exited the shuttle before standing. Wade rested his hand in the curve above her waist, the gesture simple yet poignant.

"We'd like to go back tomorrow," he said to Alex before they disembarked. "Can the shuttle drop us off at any location in town?"

"If we are not busy, sure, or you can request transportation." Alex handed a small card to Wade. "Just dial this extension."

"Thanks. Have a good evening." Wade stepped down first, extending a hand to steady Sherry as she stepped off the minibus.

"See you tomorrow." Alex waved at them and then pulled away.

They joined the foursome waiting near the entrance.

"What does everyone have planned for tomorrow?" Mike McMann asked "We're signed up for horseback riding. Although people assume all Texans are cowboys, I've never been on a horse."

"I'm spending the entire day at the spa." Genevieve patted her husband's cheek fondly. "Rupert is on his own."

"Don't worry about me," the Frenchman said. "Steel Foster is giving me a private tour so we can talk wine and grapes."

"What about you two?" Genevieve's eyes were bright with curiosity.

Ignoring the flush heating her cheeks, Sherry exchanged looks with Wade. He gave a short nod.

"Wade and I are going into town for lunch. Maybe a little shopping. I've never been to California before so I'm eager to explore the area." A tremor of anticipation ran through her. "Plus, I want to find gifts for my kids."

"No shopping for me." Mike gave an exaggerated yawn. "I'm ready to hit the hay."

"It's been a long day," Genevieve agreed, tucking her hand into the crook of her husband's arm. *"Bonne nuit."*

As the other couples wandered off, Sherry turned to Wade. "Are you tired?"

"No." He grinned down at her, the smile fading as the mood between them shifted. "I'm oddly invigorated, as if the evening is just getting started. How about you?"

"Not sleepy." She inhaled, gathering courage. "How about a nightcap? The bar is still open. Or I could make coffee."

"If I have another drink, I will fall asleep." Wade took her hand. "Coffee sounds good."

They didn't speak again until they reached her cottage. Sherry fumbled in her small handbag to find her keycard and hoped Wade didn't see her hands were shaking.

"Let me help." Wade took her purse and propped it open so the porch light shone on it, making it easier to locate the small plastic rectangle.

"Thank you."

She got the door open, flicked on a table lamp, and kicked off her heels. Padding into the kitchen, she poured water into the coffeemaker and scooped the exclusive resort grounds into the basket. The rich aroma added a homey ambiance to the luxurious interior.

"How do you take your coffee?" She turned, almost crashing into Wade who was leaning against the counter.

"Two creams. No sugar."

The gruff undertone to his words felt like a finger being trailed down her spine. She shivered, every cell in her body responding to Wade as if pulled by a magnetic force.

On the way back to her cottage, she'd realized she'd just

invited a man back to her room, yet she'd no idea of what to expect once they crossed the threshold and closed the door. They'd been alone before but never like this. Not with the air around them sparking with awareness, growing thick and heavy as the attraction escalated.

As much as Sherry wanted Wade's arms embracing her, his expressive mouth capturing hers in a kiss, his hands caressing her arms and shoulders, she longed to strengthen their emotional connection first. She wanted to know more about him, learn what was in his heart, discover what inspired him, what made him happy, what troubled him, and what he wanted in life.

"I don't know how to do this." She laid her hand on his chest, then stepped back. "I'm drawn to you, Wade. You're the first man I've been attracted to since John died. I never considered the possibility that I would fall for someone after losing my husband."

"Is that what's happening?" Wade cupped her jaw in his hand.

"I think so," she whispered. "It feels like it could be the start of something real."

"But it's complicated." He dropped his hand and twisted away. "Where are the coffee mugs?"

The change in topic jarred her for a second, but then she realized Wade was downshifting. The intensity of her admission had revved the tension between them.

"The cupboard to the left. Spoons are in the drawer next to the sink." She bent into the refrigerator for creamer.

She poured the coffee, watching Wade stir his until it was just the right shade of creamy brown. She drank hers black. Wade walked into the living room area and lowered into one of the plush chairs while she curled up at one end of the sofa.

The silence blared like a siren between them, but she forced herself to give Wade time to gather his thoughts.

"I felt something the moment we met on the shuttle at the airport," he said slowly. "Like you, I've been focused on work, but the first time we met in person I felt a connection. After the divorce, work was my distraction. It gave me a sense of purpose, and I felt that even though I'd failed my sons, I could advocate for my employees. I could make a difference for them."

"You haven't dated since your divorce?" Sherry asked.

"No." His mouth quirked into a rueful smile. "I'm not interested in starting a second family with a woman half my age. I also don't want to repeat the mistakes I've already made. But when I met you…"

"Initially, our working relationship seemed like the biggest obstacle." Sherry sipped her coffee. "Now, I feel like that will eventually be resolved."

"True." He leaned back in his chair. "You mentioned quitting, but I'd stick around if I were you. Flannigan may still recommend job cuts to the board, and that means severance packages."

"You make a good point."

"However, that doesn't eliminate the other issues standing between us, like you living in Des Moines," he stated.

"And your life is in Denver." She swallowed another gulp, the hot brew scorching the roof of her mouth. The physical pain did little to ease the anguish scalding her insides.

"Cart before the horse?" Wade set his mug aside and rested his elbows on the chair arms.

"Yes, maybe we are getting ahead of ourselves," she agreed. "But there's no sense in starting something that has no future."

"You're a good problem solver. There must be a solution we both can live with." Wade leaned forward, his expression earnest. "Many couples successfully negotiate long-distance relationships. You said you don't know how to do this. Neither do I. We can figure it out together. What I do know is that relationships take time. You start slow and build up to something...deeper, something permanent. Along the way, you work out all those sticky issues that feel insurmountable in the beginning."

"It's hard not to worry about the big things." She huddled deeper into the sofa, feeling vulnerable and exposed.

"You lost your husband." Wade's voice rang with compassion. "That's huge. Your entire life was upended. I'm sure making the necessary adjustments felt like an impossible challenge at the time, but you worked your way through it. Quite successfully, I might add." He pointed to the crystal awards on the kitchenette counter.

"You're very persuasive, Mr. Briggs." She laughed, encouraged by his positivity.

"There are no guarantees in life, Sherry. You know that better than anyone. But I already care for you. Deeply. You touched something in my heart." He leaned back in the chair as if exhausted by revealing his emotions. "Let's start slow. Get to know each other better and have some fun together."

"That sounds like a good place to start."

"How about we start now?" He picked up the remote control and turned on the TV. "What kind of movies do you like?"

"Romantic comedies. Hollywood classics. Nothing gory or scary."

He joined her on the sofa, urging her to snuggle next to him. Nestling beneath his arm felt like coming home.

"You seriously want to watch a movie?" she asked, amused and confused.

"No," he drawled. "I want to make out like teenagers, but I don't trust myself to stop. You're so beautiful, Sherry. I want to share everything with you, but it's too soon for that."

His respect made her feel cherished and adored. Her body tingled and ached, but she didn't want sex. She wanted to make love with Wade...when the time was right. That didn't mean they couldn't kiss.

"I'm not ready to go all the way," she agreed, "but can't we take another step? What about a kiss?"

"Just a kiss?" His brows lifted in amusement.

"Or three." She shifted so she was sprawled across his chest, her face turned up to his. She tugged the clip from her hair, so it fell over her shoulders.

"Sherry." Wade groaned and tunneled his fingers through the strands. He lowered his mouth to hers, feathering his lips over hers in a teasing caress.

She wound her arm around his neck, lips parting so he could deepen the kiss. Her eyes closed, fireworks exploding behind the lids as his tongue delivered the taste of love and seduction and adoration. Her senses assembled the sensory input into a collage of textures, sounds, scents, and flavors that represented Wade's essence.

Coffee, wine, salty air, the timbre of his voice, the crisp cotton of his shirt, the firm muscles in his chest and shoulders.

The kiss went on for several long moments, a leisurely exploration neither wanted to rush. Wade finally pulled away, kissing the corner of her mouth, her nose, her eyes, and then resting his forehead against hers.

"I want more," he growled. "But that will have to do for now."

Sherry felt breathless, as if she'd run a mile along the beach. She, too, wanted more. Lots more.

"How about 'Steel Magnolias?'" He paused, ready to move to another channel if she wanted to watch something different.

"One of my favorites." She sank into Wade's heat,

knowing she wouldn't remember anything about the evening except the wonderful sensation of her body pressed against his.

But what was going to happen when they both woke up tomorrow and had to face reality?

Chapter 16

*W*ade and Sherry stood outside Eden's Soap Company, admiring the late morning sunshine glinting off the window display. Colorful handmade soaps were arranged on an antique washstand holding a bowl and pitcher decorated with a faded blue floral design.

"I'm not sure about a shop of my own," Sherry murmured. "That's a big step. From the research Alison did, many people start by selling their products on Etsy or at local craft fairs. I'm already signed up for three festivals happening this summer in Des Moines."

"You don't have to make a commitment today." The skin on his arms prickled with excitement over the idea of committing himself to the woman next to him. "There's time to explore your options."

She frowned at his statement. "I have a hard time believing that."

"I understand." He shifted closer, wanting to reassure her but not pressure her. As urgently as he wanted Sherry, as much as he wanted to declare his feelings, he wanted both of them to be sure about a future together. He also wanted to savor each phase of discovery, peeling away her layers to reveal the core of her heart and soul.

John Kline had already experienced that privilege. Wade wanted to be worthy of Sherry. From this day forward, he intended to be the only man in Sherry's life, and he was willing to compromise in order to make her happy.

"Grasping each second for fear of losing it is just as bad as always putting things off for another day." He gave in and pressed a kiss to her temple. "We might not get as far down the path of life strolling along but think of what we miss if we're always running and scrambling."

"You have a nice way of framing things." She leaned against him with a small sigh of contentment. "Since John's death, I always feel like I'm in a hurry. That if I wait, even a second, I might lose time with the people I love."

"There no such thing as *enough* when it comes to the important people in our lives." He swallowed around the lump in his throat at all the moments he'd missed with Kip and Luke. Unlike Sherry who would never have more time with John, Wade had an opportunity to build new memories and new connections with his sons.

"Would you like to go in?" Wade asked.

Sherry squared her shoulders and twisted the bronze doorknob. A small bell tinkled, announcing their entrance.

A middle-aged woman with copper-red hair stood behind the counter. She gave them a welcoming smile. "Good afternoon and welcome. I'm Eden Montgomery. Are you local or just visiting?"

"We're guests at the Silver Fox Resort," Sherry said, offering their first names to the shop owner.

"Feel free to browse," Eden said, handing Sherry a small wicker basket. "If you have any questions, just ask."

Wade trailed behind Sherry as she inspected rough-hewn

bars of fragrant soap, sniffed bottles of lotion, shampoo, body wash, and other beauty products. She added a few items to the basket and then returned to the counter to complete her purchase.

"Making organic products has been my passion for years. Life interrupted, though, and I've only recently resumed my hobby. I'm thinking about going full-time and turning it into a small business." Sherry looked around the shop, obviously impressed and a bit overwhelmed. "I'm not sure where to start. Do you have any suggestions?"

"Would you like a tour?" Eden tucked the products into a bag imprinted with the shop's logo and handed it to Sherry, along with her credit card and a receipt.

"Really?" She looked at Wade, excitement lighting her eyes. "That would be fantastic."

Eden propped up a sign next to the cash register that read "Ring Bell for Assistance" and rounded the counter. "This way."

She led them through a door at the back of the shop that connected to a spacious, brightly lit workroom. A wide steel table stood in the center of the room with additional work surfaces and two deep, industrial-size sinks along the perimeter. Metal shelves held bins and plastic containers, each neatly labeled. Beeswax. Distilled Water. Coconut oil. Essential oils. Another rack held molds and empty glass vials and bottles.

"You make everything inhouse?" Sherry wandered through the work area, inhaling deeply.

Wade mimicked her but could only identify a few components perfuming the air—lemon, lavender, eucalyptus.

"Yes. All of the Eden products are handcrafted with natural and organic elements." The shop owner smiled. "That's one of our selling points. I apprenticed with a soap maker in Los Angeles before moving up here and opening my own store. She began outsourcing the manufacturing, which compromised the quality of her merchandise. People are willing to pay more for authentic artisan products. In a way, our soaps and lotions and perfumes are works of art. We put as much effort into crafting our creations as someone who works with textiles or ceramics."

"Where would you recommend starting?" Sherry's brows dipped as she focused her attention on the older woman.

"Treat it like a business from day one. Develop your branding. Identify your target market. Obtain a business license or register as a legal entity. Draft up a budget and set benchmark goals." Eden folded her arms and leaned an ample hip against the worktable. "Too many people start with unrealistic expectations and get discouraged when their products don't sell. You need to plan for success."

"That shouldn't be difficult for you." Wade grinned at Sherry, then added for Eden's benefit, "She's the best project manager at the company she works for."

"You're her boyfriend," Eden teased. "You have to say that."

Sherry flushed, the pink so appealing against her glowing skin and golden-brown curls.

"No, really. She is the best project manager. She was named corporate employee of the year. We're celebrating with a stay at the Silver Fox Resort."

"Ah. Tell Zoey and Nate I said hello. They're one of my biggest clients."

"So, it's your products I'm enjoying," Sherry mused.

"Possibly." Eden shrugged nonchalantly. "The Fosters patronize many of the cottage industries in the region. I'm not the only one who produces organic skin care and bath products."

"I appreciate your kindness in sharing advice and giving

us a tour of your workshop." Sherry took a final look around. "We should let you get back to work."

"Just a second." Eden riffled through a small box. She pulled out a handful of blank tags—rustic brown cardstock affixed to pink and brown raffia—and added them to the bag containing Sherry's purchases. "It's the small details that make a business stand out. I hire a local teen to handwrite all my labels."

"What a great idea." Sherry's smile widened.

They followed Eden back to the front of the store where a couple of women were browsing. She greeted them by name and then wished Sherry good luck.

"Be sure to come by again if you return to the resort. You're always welcome." Eden waved as they exited the shop.

"What do you think?" Wade asked, guiding her along the sidewalk.

"My head is spinning with ideas." She curved her hand around his arm and squeezed. "I already knew it would take enormous effort. That I can't just have fun concocting recipes. I need a strategy. I need something that will make my products different from all the other handcrafted soaps and lotions available to shoppers."

"What about targeting older women? Creating a line of products specifically for women over forty. You received so many compliments at the cocktail party, and everyone was amazed when you said you used your own formulations." Wade admired her smooth, youthful complexion. He loved her wholesome appeal.

"That's a wonderful idea." She gave a little hop of excitement. "I have so much work to do before even considering launching my business. Do you think six months is long enough to do all my market research, create an inventory, and put all the pieces in place that Eden recommended? If I stayed on with Stallion while setting everything up, I could invest the bonus in my business instead of using it to pay living expenses while I get things up and running."

"Spoken like a true project manager." His stomach clenched as her words reminded him he still had to deal with Flannigan. They had a meeting scheduled for four—right before Flannigan and his wife departed for the return trip to Australia. After leaving Sherry's cottage at midnight, he'd stayed up another two hours going over his proposal. He was ready to appeal to Flannigan's greed but still worried the CEO would flat-out reject him on principle: It wasn't Flannigan's idea.

Wade wanted to be satisfied with the fact he'd done everything possible to save jobs within the North American division. He wasn't a miracle worker, and the final decision wasn't up to him.

Still...his people needed their jobs. Sherry needed her job for at least another six months.

"Want to get something to eat?" She pointed toward a tavern on the next block. "April and I went there for karaoke a couple nights ago. It's known for its blue cheese burgers and sweet potato fries."

Wade wasn't hungry, his stomach a roiling mass of nerves, but he wouldn't pass up the opportunity to spend time with this woman. He wanted to share all his future moments with her.

As they entered the rustic restaurant and bar, he reminded himself of the advice he'd given Sherry last night and felt a modicum of relief.

We can figure it out together.

Chapter 17

$\mathcal{I}$t was close to three by the time Sherry and Wade returned to the resort.

She thanked Alex for shuttling them back and forth to town. Wade handed Alex a twenty, and then they entered the lobby, shoulder to shoulder but not holding hands as they'd done in town.

"Do you want to rehearse your presentation one more time?" Sherry had sensed a change in Wade's demeanor as they neared the resort. His hands were fisted, his jaw clenched, shoulders hunched forward. He probably had the information memorized, but she was trying to distract him.

He pulled a thin sheaf of papers from the back pocket of his khakis. "I reviewed my notes while you were trying on dresses at that little boutique. I'm glad you bought that one with the violet lace overlay. It was made for you."

"Thanks. It will probably find its way into Alison's closet, but I don't mind. She loaned me most of the clothing I packed for this—"

"Stuart?" Wade's abrupt interruption prompted Sherry to turn around.

Stuart and Caroline Flannigan were leading a procession of bellhops and luggage carts through the lobby.

"Oh, Sherry. I'm so glad to see you." Caroline rushed over and hugged her. "I was afraid I wouldn't be able to say goodbye. And thank you."

"I thought you weren't leaving until later this afternoon." Sherry cast a confused look between Caroline, her husband, and Wade.

"Our schedule changed." The CEO ignored Wade, whose face was darkening with rage.

"But you agreed to meet with Mr. Briggs at four o'clock." Sherry felt her own temper ignite.

"You didn't say anything about a meeting, Stuart." Caroline pushed her sunglasses to the top of her head, her tone chiding. "I'm so sorry, Mr. Briggs. Would it be an inconvenience for you to meet with my husband now? We still have a few minutes."

"Caroline—" Flannigan scowled a warning at his wife.

"Mr. Briggs and Mrs. Kline have gone out of their way to accommodate our requests and make our stay pleasant, *Stuart.*" Caroline mimicked her husband's tone and glared at him. "If you agreed to meet with Mr. Briggs—Wade—then you should honor that commitment. Keeping promises is one of your father's highest values. We're flying home on a private jet, for Pete's sake. It's not like we're going to miss our flight."

Sherry did a double take, realizing more than just Caroline's makeup and fashion had changed. At some point in the last few days, the woman discovered she had a backbone. Her admiration for Caroline went up several notches. This was a woman with integrity and decency. Sherry suspected her marriage to Stuart wouldn't last long once she faced the truth about her husband's true character.

"Fine. If it means that much to you." Mr. Flannigan

scanned the lobby and seemed to realize they were drawing curious stares, some of them from Stallion employees. "Martin, get our luggage loaded. This won't take long." He stalked over to the registration desk where Amy Denham was working. "I need a private office for a few minutes."

"Uh, certainly, Mr. Flannigan." Amy quickly masked her shock at the rude demand. "Our catering office is unoccupied. Let me escort you there."

Amy led the two men down a short hall, while Sherry and Caroline stood awkwardly in the middle of the lobby as the bellhops shuttled the luggage out the front entrance.

"Let's sit down while we're waiting." Sherry pointed to a cluster of chairs near the massive stone fireplace.

"I'm embarrassed by my husband's behavior." Caroline fidgeted in her seat, fingers wrapped tightly around the handle of her cherry red patent leather Dior handbag. "He's been rude to virtually everyone, and now this."

"How long have you been married?" Sherry asked gently.

"Six months. It was a whirlwind romance, or so I thought." Caroline's mouth and shoulders drooped with unhappiness. "Stuart can be quite charming…when it suits him."

"I'm sorry." Sherry covered Caroline's icy fingers with her hand. "You're a very special person, and I'm glad we had the opportunity to become friends."

"Really?" Caroline's eyes widened. "You're not just saying that because I'm married to the CEO of the company you work for? We're really friends?"

"Of course." Sherry reared back in surprise. Was that how things worked in Caroline's world? "It wouldn't matter if you were married to the janitor. Although, if Wade can't convince your husband not to sell off poor-performing units, I may not be with Stallion for long."

"What do you mean?" Caroline's elegant pale-blond

brows dipped in concern. "You were just named corporate Employee of the Year. Why would your job be in jeopardy?"

"Not just my job." Sherry was too frustrated to hold her tongue. Besides, Caroline was married to the CEO. She must be privy to corporate operations at the highest level. "Your husband is supposed to make a recommendation to the board of directors at the next meeting about North American division operations. Some of the units, mine included, have had higher than usual losses because of natural disaster claims. It isn't poor management or wasteful spending. There have been discussions with a competitor about selling off these units for a more favorable profit margin. Wade developed an alternative solution that would save jobs and bring in additional earnings, but the turnaround would take six to twelve months."

"And my husband doesn't want to wait that long." Caroline's eyes hardened as she clamped her teeth together. "He always has been rather impatient."

"I'm done, Briggs." Flannigan's loud voice breeched the serenity of the mostly empty lobby. "You have my answer." He strode across the tiled floor, angrily gesturing toward his wife.

Wade followed, his mouth a grim slash, posture rigid, hands fisted around the sheaf of papers he'd rolled into a tube.

"Well, that's that." He stared at Sherry, his eyes flat like two coins.

"Caroline, I said we're leaving." Flannigan stood at the front desk, hands on hips.

"Is that the proposal?" Caroline whispered.

Sherry nodded.

Caroline plucked the paper from Wade's white-knuckled grip and tucked it into her bag. Curving an arm around

Sherry, she leaned in for a final hug. "Let me see what I can do."

Sherry watched the couple leave and then turned to Wade.

He stood frozen in place, his face expressionless.

"Wade?" Sherry peered up at him. "Are you okay?"

"No," he hissed. "What is it about this place? Every time I come here, I fail at something. First, it was my marriage. I brought Juliet here for our anniversary, and she told me she was having an affair. This time, I've failed to protect my employees. Flannigan is recommending that the company sell off more than thirty percent of the North American units. Not only will hundreds of people be out of jobs, but if the board accepts his recommendation, they'll lose significant market share."

"Unbelievable." Sherry shook her head in disbelief. Was Stuart Flannigan really so arrogant as to assume the experienced business leaders sitting on the company's board of directors wouldn't be able to see the downside to his self-serving recommendation? "The profit losses are happening on his watch."

"He also mentioned recommending an extensive restructuring to position the company for 'growth in foreign markets.'"

"Did he really say that?" Sherry laughed bitterly.

"Yes." Wade shook his head as if to clear his thoughts. "I'm sorry, Sherry. I really thought I could convince Flannigan to hold on to our employees. I don't know how fast his plan will roll out, but I'd start working on finding something else right away."

"Don't worry about me." Sherry hated the haunted look in Wade's eyes. "Maybe there's still something we can do. Maybe you can hire a company to help displaced employees find jobs. The staff will need to create resumes. Many will need to practice their interviewing skills."

"Again, you amaze me." He stared down at her. "In a matter of months, you'll be out of a job, yet you're worried about everyone else and already have a plan to minimize the impact."

"You would have suggested it yourself if you weren't reeling from Flannigan's condescension." Sherry didn't want the CEO's decision to undermine Wade's confidence as a leader. His influence only went so far, but he'd stretched far beyond those limits. "What do we do now?"

"*You* enjoy the rest of your stay at the resort." Wade grasped her shoulders in his hands, his voice authoritative. "I…I can't stay. I can't mingle with our people and pretend everything is fine. I can't stand knowing they're headed into bad news when they report back to work. You're right. I might not be able to save their jobs, but I can organize resources to make the transition less difficult."

"You're…leaving?" First came fiery incredulity, then icy fear. "What about *us*?"

Bleak. That was the only word to describe Wade's expression as he slowly shook his head. "I can't. Not now."

"You've fulfilled your obligation to your employees, Wade." Sherry gripped his fingers, but they remained limp. "There's nothing else you can do."

"I know. I've failed you all." He choked out the words. "I need to go."

He yanked his hands free…and walked away.

Sherry's heart felt like it was being crushed. That was the second time Wade had walked away, and she vowed there wouldn't be a third.

Chapter 18

 *ne Week Later*

"Sherry, you have a call on line one." Juanita, the front desk secretary for the Des Moines office, waved at her as she returned from lunch. "The insistent woman has called three times in the past hour but won't give her name or provide a callback number."

"Okay. Let me get back to my desk and then transfer the call." She exhaled wearily and forced herself to hurry through the labyrinth of cubicles to her small office. The light was already blinking on her phone, so she dropped her lunch bag and purse onto her chair and lifted the handset.

"Hello. This is Sherry Kline. May I ask who's calling?"

"Hi, Sherry. It's Caroline Flannigan."

The woman sounded excited.

"Hi, Caroline. I'm so glad to hear from you, but what a surprise. How are you? I've been thinking about you." *And worried, because you're married to such a jerk.*

She leaned against the office door, her line of sight focusing on the bookshelf where her two crystal awards were displayed. Gazing at them, she felt zero joy, zero sense of accomplishment. Stuart Flannigan and Stallion's board of directors' decision to terminate more than four hundred talented, hardworking employees demonstrated zero appreciation for their contributions to the company. The awards were worthless.

She, at least, had a $25,000 safety net. Her coworkers were not so lucky, but none of them knew it yet.

"I want to give you a heads up. There are huge changes coming to Stallion." Caroline's secretive whisper made Sherry wary. "The board has a press conference scheduled for Monday. I want you to be there. Can you come?"

"What?" Sherry screeched, clapping her hand over her mouth to prevent another outburst. "You mean to Australia?"

"Yes. Do you have a passport?" Caroline's tone shifted, and she suddenly sounded mature and confident. "I can't send the private jet for you, but I can book a first-class ticket."

"Y-y-yes, I have a passport..." She and John had completed the process, but he never had a chance to use his. Hers was tucked away in a file drawer at home, still awaiting its first travel stamp. "I can't just leave to travel halfway around the world. I'm still working. I doubt my boss will give me the time off."

"Don't worry. The trip has already been cleared with your boss. That's why I've been calling. I wanted to speak with you before Mr. Bivens did."

"Is there a problem? Why am I needed at headquarters?" Confusion made Sherry hold the phone a little tighter as she waited for an answer.

"I can't give you details over the phone," Caroline

whispered. "Trust me. You'll want to be here when the fireworks start. Will you come?"

"I don't—" Sherry looked at the stack of files in her inbox and reminded herself she'd planned to begin experimenting with a new soap recipe over the weekend.

"Wade Briggs is here." Caroline dangled the one carrot Sherry found hard to resist, but the offer didn't change the fact Wade had walked away from her—twice. Besides that, he hadn't called, texted, or emailed, and when Kimberly called to thank Sherry for her help and report her grandmother was recovering nicely, she, too, dodged Sherry's casual questions about her boss.

If she wasn't head over heels for Wade, she'd be spitting mad.

"Does he know you're asking me to fly down there?"

"Nope." Caroline's smug response echoed across the phone line.

"One question. *If* I fly down there, will my being there help save jobs?"

"Possibly."

"Then I'll take the chance."

Caroline's exuberant squeal almost pierced Sherry's eardrum. She laughed, the same sense of excitement flooding her veins, although she didn't know what she was getting excited about.

"I'll email confirmation once your flight is booked." Caroline paused. "I owe you so much, Sherry."

"Me? Why?" The confusion circling again rebounded.

"You showed me what type of person I want to be, and I'm grateful to have met you when I did."

"I feel the same." Sherry drew in a long breath. "I guess I'll see you in a few days."

"I can't wait." Caroline disconnected the call.

Sherry placed the headset into the holder, still confused.

She'd just agreed to drop everything and fly to Australia. She wished she knew why, because if it involved Wade, she should be running in the opposite direction. At least, that's what her head was telling her.

Her heart had a different opinion.

~

"Australia?" Alison stood in the kitchen of Sherry's trilevel, jaw hanging open in surprise. "When?"

"I leave tonight. They just sent me my tickets. I'm traveling first-class. Can you believe it?"

Alison moved a little closer. "Why? Did something happen in California?"

"Nothing that would require me to travel to Australia. Why?"

"I don't know. You seem different...more confident."

"Is that a bad thing?" Sherry poured a second glass of Chardonay and handed it to her daughter who took a fortifying sip.

"No." Alison slid onto a stool, resting her chin in her palm as she raked an assessing look up and down Sherry. "I just want to understand. I've been after you for months to reconnect with friends, travel, get back to gardening, do something with your organic products, or go out with a nice man. For months, all I've heard is one excuse after another, but suddenly you're video chatting with friends in Paris and Dallas, and now you're jetting off to Sydney. You've applied to the Women's Entrepreneur Mentorship program, and I've overheard you mention a guy. Wayne, I think it is."

"Wade," Sherry corrected, her mouth curving helplessly into a smile. *Ah, Wade.* She would see him in less than seventy-two hours.

"Wade." Alison's eyes widened as she connected the dots. "Wade, as in Mr. Briggs, your boss."

"He's technically not my boss. He's the president of Stallion's North American division."

"Yet, your face lights up when you talk about him. Did you guys do the funky monkey?"

"Alison Arlene Kline! What kind of question is that?" Sherry's hand flew to her chest, right over her pounding heart.

"You're a modern woman, Mom. You're allowed to have a little fun." Alison held out her wine glass for a fill up. "You'd better top me off. I want to hear this story."

"At the risk of sounding like a prude, I don't have sex on first dates, or second dates for that matter." *At least not yet*, she amended silently.

"But you did have a date with Wade." Alison took a slow sip of wine. "Is Wade the reason you're going to Australia?"

For a second, Alison sounded like a little girl who needed reassurance that everything would be okay. Sherry hadn't heard that plaintive note in her daughter's voice since John died. She realized that despite all her daughter's urging that she move on and leave the past behind, part of Alison feared too much change, or possibly that Sherry would leave her behind as well—which would never happen.

Her first impulse was to reassure Alison, but her daughter was a grown woman. She needed to learn strength and resilience. Sherry prayed life would be kind to Alison, but there were no guarantees. It was better that she be honest and open, and then support her daughter as best she could.

"He's one of the reasons." Sherry leaned her elbows on the counter across from Alison, knitting her fingers together. "Caroline, a woman I met in California, called and invited me. It has to do with the company, but she wasn't at liberty to share all of the details. There's a big announcement coming on Monday."

"And it involves you?"

Sherry shrugged. "I don't know."

"I still don't understand, but you sound certain about this." Alison twirled her wineglass, still upset.

"There are so many things in life that aren't certain, honey. I thought I'd have years and years with your father. I thought my job with Stallion was secure. I thought the corporate trip would be miserable. Wrong, wrong, and wrong again. The only thing I'm sure of is that I don't want to waste a moment of whatever time I have remaining." Sherry rounded the counter and wrapped Alison in her arms, slowly rocking back and forth. "I love you, Alison. That will never change, no matter what."

"I love you, too, Mom. I'm so proud of you."

Sherry laughed, smoothing a strand of auburn hair out of her daughter's face. "What for? I'm just following your advice."

"Better late than never." Alison raised her glass in a toast. "Finish your wine. We have another trip to pack for, and this time we're going shopping. No excuses."

Chapter 19

"You're here!" Caroline's effusive welcome slammed into Sherry the minute the elevator doors slid open, revealing the private foyer leading to the forty-million-dollar penthouse overlooking Sydney Harbour.

She barely recognized the younger woman.

Caroline had put on a few pounds, the fullness much more flattering than her stick-thin figure. Her hair had been cut and colored so it fell in natural waves just below her shoulders, and it was almost impossible to tell she was wearing makeup. Barefoot, dressed in jeans and a thick cream-colored sweater that dipped off one shoulder, Caroline could have definitely passed now as one of Alison's college chums.

"My gosh, Caroline." Sherry returned her embrace, amazed at the transformation. "What happened?"

"Oh, you mean this?" Caroline flipped one wrist as if holding a tray of drinks, the other planted on her cocked hip. "Let's just say it's been an eventful week."

"You need to fill me in on everything." Sherry rolled her suitcase out of the way and wandered over to the floor-to-ceiling windows showcasing a stunning view of downtown Sydney.

"Let's go out onto the terrace." Caroline picked up a phone, pressed a button, and ordered food from whoever answered. "We don't have a lot of time. We have to be at the corporate office in three hours. You have enough time to eat something, grab a power nap, and dress."

"I slept on the plane. I'll be fine until bedtime."

"Mm-hm. That's what I said the first time I flew from the US. Your sleep schedule is going to be messed up for weeks. And by the way, I go by Caro. Stuart was the only one who called me Caroline." Caroline—Caro— pressed a button, and the glass slider opened with a whoosh, cool air rushing into the spacious penthouse. "If you're uncomfortable, I can have Lance turn on the heaters. It's only supposed to get into the lower seventies today."

"I'm fine," Sherry said again. "Details. I need details!"

"This is your first trip down under, right?" Caro grinned mischievously and pointed to an arched structure spanning the water. "That's the Sydney Harbour Bridge. To the right, you'll see the Opera House. You're looking at the Circular Quay, also known as the gateway to Sydney. Come for the holidays, and you'll have the best seat in the house for the New Year's Eve fireworks show."

"Caro." Sherry intentionally used her friend's new name. "You can play tour guide later. I've been going crazy wondering what's going on."

A plump young woman appeared with a tray of food, further delaying Caro's big reveal. Sherry tamped down her impatience as the assistant served fresh juice, steaming coffee, croissants, slices of cheese and ham, and a tropical fruit salad.

"Eat." Caro shoved a juicy slice of kiwi into her mouth.

Sherry smiled at the older women in a black and white uniform who handed her a cup of coffee. She bit into a croissant and chewed slowly, taking in Caroline's vast change. Fortunately, the new relaxed state convinced Caro to stop teasing and get down to business.

"Stuart is no longer CEO of Stallion Protection Partners." Caro forked up a chunk of mango and waved it around like a magic wand. "And," she said with a sly grin, "Stuart is also on the search for wife number six."

"You filed for divorce?" Sherry forgot the delicious food on her plate.

"My attorney is working on it. It will take some time, but at least I'm not prolonging my error. I have you to thank for that."

Sherry hated the thought that she was responsible for a broken marriage, except that Caro looked healthy and happy and Stuart Flannigan was, in Wade's words, a horse's ass.

"Go back to the beginning." Sherry inhaled the rich coffee aroma before taking another sip.

"Sorry." Caro chewed the mango and swallowed, then laid down her fork. "It's been hectic. Let me start again." She folded her legs, hands on her knees as the faint sounds of city life rose up to the penthouse terrace. "On the flight back from San Francisco, I asked Stuart about Wade's proposal. He didn't know I'd already read the report. He bragged that he was going to make the company several billion dollars by selling off a third of the North American units, which would net him a high seven-figure bonus.

"When I asked why he was opposed to Wade's proposal, which would net a similar profit, he explained his bonuses are based on annual numbers, and the money wouldn't come in soon enough. I pointed out the long-term potential for profit was higher if the company retained employees, and he got angry. His behavior got abusive to the point that I locked myself in the master suite for the rest of the flight and contacted my father-in-law, Reginald Flannigan. When we landed, Reggie met us at the airport. He asked if I needed a doctor, set up an appointment with the best divorce attorney in Sydney, and whisked Stuart off to the family estate in Kiwirrkurra."

"I hope Stuart didn't hurt you." She inventoried Caro's face but saw no injuries.

"I'm smarter than people give me credit for." Caro flipped her hair over her shoulder. "Playing the bimbo doesn't create a good first impression, but I put myself through college and graduated with an MBA."

"Wow, that is impressive." *I had no idea.*

"Wade's proposal is brilliant. I emailed Wade and asked him to send me the full details. The plan will make the company twice as much money as the recommendation Stuart was going to give to the board. I'm not sure what Reggie plans to do with Stuart, but his days with Stallion are over. There's an internal investigation underway, and all of Stuart's financial transactions since he's been in charge are being audited."

"Your father-in-law sounds like a good man."

"Reggie's the best." Caro smiled. "He's like the father I never had. He insisted Stuart sign over the penthouse and ordered a very generous divorce settlement. Stuart can keep his plane and yacht. Now, I can do anything or go anywhere, and I don't need a man to make it happen. That's all because of you, Sherry."

"I don't know about that. You stood up for yourself, and that takes guts."

"But you didn't make fun of me or use me or judge me, like so many others have. When I heard how you lost your husband and bounced back from that, you inspired me. I wasn't planning to divorce Stuart until he tried to backhand me. I figured if you had the courage to rebuild your life, I could do the same."

Tears filled Sherry's eyes. So many days, she'd gone through the motions of living, not for herself but for Alison and Tyler. She never set out to be a role model or hero. She just did what needed to be done. Knowing she'd inspired Caro to make a difficult choice and reach deep for courage to change her life was worth a hundred times more than her Employee of the Year awards.

"I'm glad I could help." Sherry got up and held Caro tightly.

One day, she hoped to introduce Alison to the new Caro. They would like each other. She pulled back, remembering one loose end that hadn't yet been resolved. "You said Wade is here. Where does he fit into all of this?"

Caro wiped her cheeks. "When I showed Wade's proposal to my father-in-law, he asked Wade to fly down since he's the brains behind one of the most pivotal strategies to come before the board in a decade. Not only has Wade found a way to turn around those huge losses stemming from hurricanes, floods, and forest fires, his proposal has the potential to increase market share and profitability by double digits."

"So, the board is going to approve his plan? One swipe and all those jobs are off the chopping block?" She held her breath, waiting for Caro's answer.

"Yes. Your job is secure, Sherry. Even better, Reggie wants Wade to replace Stuart as CEO. He made an official offer yesterday. He's asked Wade to make a decision before the press conference."

Wade? CEO of Stallion?

He'd be required to move to Australia.

What about his boys?

What about her?

"That's why you're here, Sherry." Wade's familiar voice dragged her back from the edge of the chaotic thoughts spiraling through her head.

Had she asked those questions aloud?

She rose on shaking knees. "This is crazy." She glanced between Caro and Wade, settling her eyes on him as emotion swelled through her.

Dressed in a tailored black pinstripe suit with a snowy white shirt and dark red tie, he looked more like a CEO than Stuart ever had. He looked fit and intelligent and successful, distinguished and trustworthy. He was the perfect man to serve as CEO of a global business. He would protect the interests of the corporation without sacrificing values and ethics. Stallion would become one of the world's most desirable companies to work for.

"You were made for this role." Sherry remained rooted in place, hardly noticing when Caro slipped back into the penthouse, leaving them alone.

"It's a job." Wade's smile was tender. He strode across the terrace until they stood a few inches apart. "It's one helluva job, yes, but at the end of my life, I don't want to look back at eighty-hour work weeks and a legacy defined by spreadsheets and shareholder reports."

"What do you want?" It took all her courage to ask.

"You. Our kids. Grandkids. Travel. Walks on the beach. Dinner with friends. Nice-smelling organic soap." He blinked, his lashes spiky with tears, and tried to lighten the mood with a bit of levity. "Three years ago, I would have said yes to Reginald's offer in a heartbeat. Everything is different now. Because of you."

"But Wade, think about the amazing things you could do for Stallion employees. You're one of the kindest, strongest, wisest leaders I know. Turning down this offer means putting my wants and needs ahead of everyone else."

"You don't have to ask for that, Sherry. Your needs and wants and desires are the only ones that matter. That's how it's supposed to be when you're in love."

"Wait." Sherry reached out to clutch Wade's hands. "Did you just say you love me?"

Chapter 20

 ne Year Later

"This is our last beach walk for a while." Wade squeezed Sherry's hand, pulling her into the surf, dampening the bottom of her rolled-up jeans. "Better enjoy it while you can."

"You make it sound like I'm taking a job as the CEO of an international corporation instead of opening a small boutique specializing in handcrafted organic bath and beauty products." She shoved him playfully, sending him into the frothy waves rolling in from the Pacific Ocean onto the beach at Silver Fox Resort.

"You are a CEO, Mrs. Briggs. Chief of Every Operation for Brave and Beautiful Organic Skin Care, LLC."

"Mrs. Sherry Briggs, CEO." She threw her arms around her husband's waist, not caring that their antics in the water was soaking them both. "I love the sound of that. Can you get a nameplate made for my office door?"

"The one already labeled 'Laundry Room?'" Wade

chuckled and steered them back to the hardpack sand beyond the surf's edge. "You're going to need more space, my love. You can't keep up with inventory demands if you're working out of a laundry room, not even one as sizable as ours."

Six months ago, Wade had flown Sherry up from Des Moines and surprised her with an engagement ring and a house-hunting trip. In less than six weeks, her house was on the market, her things being transported to a five-bedroom house, one bedroom for each kid, plus a master suite.

"I know." She sighed, meandering alongside him, taking in the stands of pines and the technicolor sunset over the sapphire ocean. "The space next to our downtown shop will be vacant next month. Alison suggested expanding into that area and converting the front to a studio where I can offer lessons and use the back as a private workspace. I just hate the thought of spending so much time away from you. I've liked working from home and letting Alison and Derek manage the store. I think Alison is a natural at running the business."

"With Derrick handling finances, inventory, marketing, and distribution, you have the time to be creative. You've got all the bases covered."

"It does seem things are working out. I love that Kip and Luke can come home for the weekends if they want. And I'm thrilled they're doing well at school, both with a 3.5 GPA."

"All that, and to think we've been married less than a week."

"It's been the best week ever." She twined her fingers with his. "The best week on top of the best year."

"How many glasses of wine did you have with dinner? You have to be drunk to describe the past twelve months as the best of anything."

"Blame it on Steel Foster. His new Chardonnay is exquisite."

"Yes, it is, and the reason I've arranged for him to send two cases to us, so pace yourself." Wade dropped onto the sand, next to their blanket and dessert basket, and tugged her down between his knees so her back rested against his chest. He wrapped his arms around her as they settled in to watch the sun set.

Twilight, just the two of them, reflecting on the day and anticipating the next had become her favorite part of their honeymoon at Silver Fox Resort. There was no noise. No distractions. No demands. Just peace and quiet and each other.

She was so blessed. She'd spent the first half of her life with a man she loved deeply who'd given her two beautiful children. And now she got to spend the last half of her life with a man she loved just as much who encouraged her to pursue her dreams, venture into the world, and welcome new family members into her life.

She curled her hands around Wade's biceps and tilted her head to look up at him. "I'm curious. What makes you say the past year was anything less than amazing?"

"Flying back and forth to Australia twice a month. Juggling Kip's and Luke's athletic events. Planning Alison and Derrick's wedding. Discovering Caro got drunk at the aforementioned wedding, had a one-night stand, and is now pregnant. Helping launch my brilliant wife's business." He pressed a kiss to the top of her head. "Should I go on?"

"You forgot about Stuart's wedding and divorce from new wife number six, and my brother's appearance on the silver fox reality dating show. I never imagined he'd run off with the producer. She's older than he is by three years." Sherry laughed, amused by all of the changes in just one year.

"But everyone is happy."

Wade was right. Everyone was happy and healthy, except maybe Stuart Flannigan but he was a lost cause.

After serving as interim CEO for Stallion until a suitable candidate was found, Wade had retired from corporate life and now worked as a consultant, but she assumed soon he would tire of making the trip to the airport from their five-bedroom, eight-thousand-square-foot home sitting on the ridge above Boulder with a brilliant view of the mountain range.

Sherry closed her eyes, welcoming memories of their private ceremony on the beach six days ago. She loved the people who enriched their lives, but she'd wanted their wedding to be intimate—just the two of them promising to love and honor and cherish each other for as much time as they had together.

The rhythmic whoosh of the waves and gentle clatter of tree limbs was the perfect soundtrack for the final night of their honeymoon. They watched the sun sink below the horizon, then strolled back to their villa in the purple twilight, Sherry needing no words to express the fullness in her heart. There were many ways to communicate affection, and she'd quickly learned her husband's love language.

"I love you, Sherry Briggs." Wade pulled her closer. "Just in case you weren't sure."

"As I love you, but it doesn't hurt to hear it anyway because we both know that we can't take a single moment for granted."

Wade reached for the open bottle of Chardonnay and poured Sherry a glass before pulling out the plate of chocolate-covered strawberries Nate had prepared for them. "Here's to second chances." Wade clinked his glass against hers.

"Here's to living life in the moment," she said, leaning back for another kiss.

He lowered his head and captured her lips. She missed seeing the sun dip below the horizon, but she didn't mind. As stunning as the sunset was, the love she shared with Wade was so much more beautiful.

I'm so glad you could join Sherry and Wade on their journey to their happily ever after.

Those of you who have read my books or been part of my newsletter have heard my explanation for why Authors never see their Star Ratings requested by Amazon, so thank you for allowing me to share the information once again.

When Amazon asks a reader to "Rate this book" on their Kindle, Amazon is the only one to see these ratings.

I'm left clueless about how you feel about this book. Your input matters.

Book reviews help me decide what kind of books I write. Plus, the more people who leave a review, the more likely Amazon is to move a book up in the rankings? Written reviews help other readers find and love a series.

Please continue to rate the book on your Kindle or reader as this helps Amazon, but take an extra moment to pop over to the review section (Book: B09GD948NV) and leave a few words!

Seriously, a few words like, "great story," is enough.

If you have not read my Elkridge Series or the Lonely

Ridge Collection, and have no idea why authors keep asking you as a reader to take a few minutes to leave even a couple of word reviews, here's the break down of how reviews work in this crazy business.

Reviews (not ratings) help authors qualify for advertising opportunities. Without triple digit reviews, an author may miss out on these valuable opportunities. And with only a "star rating" the author has little chance of participating in specific promotions, which means authors continue to struggle, and many talented writers give up writing altogether.

Readers aren't the only ones who use reviews to help make purchasing decisions. Producers and directors use your reviews when looking for new projects.

This is why I'm asking for your help.

A few kind words make such a massive difference to me. Your words give me the encouragement I need to continue writing because honestly, I write my books for you, and I'd like to keep delivering the types of stories you want to read.

And, yes, every book in a series needs reviews, not just the first book. Even if a book has been out for awhile, a fresh review can breathe new life into a book.

So, please take a few minutes to leave a short review. Even a couple of words will brighten my day.

Lastly. Thank you for reading this book. I hope to see you again soon. Cheers!

Author Notes

Dear Readers,

Sherry and Wade's story came floating to me as I watched a pair of business professionals meet in person for the first time. They seemed familiar with each other through work, and I could see by the way she leaned in and the way he looked at her, there was an attraction.

Circumstances didn't allow the couple to sit together. There were eight people at the event, but I got the impression they would have liked to get to know each other better.

Neither was wearing a wedding band, and I started thinking of all the reasons these two interesting people were not married—because that's where romance writer's minds go.

Sure, I know some people don't want to be married, or some people, men especially, don't like to wear a wedding band. But there was something about this couple that suggested being single was not their preferred status, that they had too much love left to share.

So there you have it…the inspiration for Sweet Chardonnay. When I day dream—you get a new story.

Thank you, again, for coming along this journey with me. Now, I'm off to write more words.

~Lyz

More Books By
Lyz Kelley

SILVER FOX RESORT
A sweet mature romance book set
SILVER SPOON
SILVER DOLLAR
SILVER BELLS
SWEET DECEMBER

WINE PAIRING
Sweet mature stand-alone books
SWEET CHAMPAGNE
SWEET CHARDONNAY

SECRETS
Sexy urban romance book set
BILLIONAIRE'S SECRET
DOCTOR'S SECRET

THE ELKRIDGE SERIES
Solve a mystery in books 1-4, then
revisit characters in small town USA.
BLINDED
ABANDONED
ORPHANED
RESCUED
UNMISTAKEN
ATONEMENT
BITTERSWEET
Coming soon:
GUARDED

Do you want a free book?

I've got a present for my readers, your very own ebook exclusive.

https://geni.us/LyzKelleyFreeBook

Sign up to start falling in love today!

Thank you for reading: SWEET CHARDONNAY

Award-winning author Lyz Kelley mixes a little bit of heart, healing, humanity, happiness, hope, and honor in all her books that are written especially for you.

She's is a total disaster in the kitchen, a compulsive neat freak, a tea snob, and adores writing about and falling in love with everyday heroes.

Please also consider leaving a review on Amazon Goodreads and/or BookBub. Reviews help readers find new books to read, and authors find their footing.

You can also find Lyz on Facebook and Instagram for news, contests, giveaways, and more exciting stuff!

Belvitri
Services

Copyright

Cover Art: Covers by Megan Parker